SLASH AND BURN

Visit us at www.boldstrokesbooks.com

SLASH AND BURN

by

Valerie Bronwen

A Division of Bold Strokes Books

2014

ISBN 13: 978-1-60282-986-2

THIS TRADE PAPERBACK ORIGINAL IS PUBLISHED BY
BOLD STROKES BOOKS, INC.
P.O. BOX 249
VALLEY FALLS, NY 12185

FIRST EDITION: FEBRUARY 2014

CREDITS
EDITOR: STACIA SEAMAN
PRODUCTION DESIGN: STACIA SEAMAN
COVER DESIGN BY SHERI (GRAPHICARTIST2020@HOTMAIL.COM)

This is for VAB, with love.

CHAPTER ONE

If there's a worse way to start a writers' conference than having a dead body practically land at your feet, I'd *really* rather not know what it is, thank you very much.

Despite my reputation—which in all fairness is somewhat earned—I actually *was* minding my own business when it happened. I had made dinner plans with one of my oldest and dearest friends and had just taken a seat in the inner courtyard of the Maison Maintenon, a boutique hotel in the French Quarter, to wait for him. Jerry had texted me just as I walked in the front door of the hotel to let me know he was running a little late and to wait for him by the swimming pool. I've always found tardiness to be more than a little irritating, and I despise the term "fashionably late." Since when has being rude been in fashion? But in all the years I've known him, I don't think Jerry has ever *once* been on time to meet me.

Hope always springs eternal, however. I'm always optimistic.

So, more than a little annoyed, I walked through the front door of the hotel and down the long front hallway. It was quite lovely, with a black-and-white parquet floor, high ceilings, and some amazing oil paintings on the bright-yellow walls. A huge chandelier's crystal teardrops sparkled overhead, and there were some large doors on the right wall. There was a small desk set up just before another door at the back, which I could see opened into a narrow room with a door opened to a courtyard filled with lush plants. I nodded to the older woman sitting behind the desk as I walked past. There was a sign nailed to an enormous live oak in the courtyard reading *Pool* with an arrow pointing off to the right. Once I went down the three cement steps, I could see the building continued, making an L shape around the courtyard. There was a tall brick fence to my left. I turned and walked past the ice machine in the short passage to the swimming pool.

The sparkling pool glittered in the late-afternoon sun and almost filled this interior courtyard completely. There was a cement walkway about two feet wide on the two long sides of the pool, and there was another brick fence on the other side. When I emerged from the dark passage, I could see there was a three-story building opposite the main building with a couple of iron tables and chairs set up in the shade cast by the second-floor gallery. A gate through the brick fence led to another courtyard and what appeared to be a one-story cottage back there. It was almost obnoxiously humid, and I reached into my purse for a handkerchief to blot beads of perspiration from my forehead as I walked alongside the pool to get to the shade. I gratefully slid into one of the chairs, glad to be out of the harsh early-June sun. I dug my smartphone out of my cavernous quilted shoulder bag, answered some pressing emails, and scrolled through Facebook, reading about what various online "friends" were eating or doing at their gym, when I realized Jerry was now about fifteen minutes late.

I swore under my breath. Maybe it's all the years spent teaching, but my tolerance for lateness is much lower than most people's. Okay, it's nonexistent—I'm known for locking the door when it's time for class to start, and if you aren't in your seat, too bad so sad for you.

I was firing off a strongly worded text to Jerry about his inconsideration when I heard a door open overhead, followed by an odd sound. My mind registered it as a grunt—like someone had lifted something particularly heavy. Curious, I looked up. This was immediately followed by the groan of wood—anyone who has lived in an old house knows that sound, and I've lived in plenty. There was another grunt. My curiosity growing, I pushed my chair back and started to stand up just as something large fell into my line of sight and landed with a sickening crunching sound on the cement just a few feet from where I was sitting.

I have always taken a great deal of pride in my ability to rise to every occasion, no matter what that might be. I am rarely, if ever, nonplussed, nor am I one of those people who think of the proper rejoinder hours too late for it to do any good. I am equally proud to say that over my many years I have gained a well-earned reputation for having the remarkable ability to remain calm under any circumstance and being able to think logically no matter what chaos is erupting around me. Had there been a category in my senior high school yearbook for "Most Likely to Stay Calm During a Crisis"—well, my photograph would have most deservedly been above that caption.

So, given that a body had just landed at my feet, I didn't even pause to think.

I opened my mouth and let out a bloodcurdling scream.

Maybe not the most feminist-woman-in-control reaction, I thought as it echoed off the brick walls on every side of the courtyard and I began to regain my composure, *but I defy anyone not to scream under these circumstances.*

I took a few deep breaths to finish clearing my head and to help get my racing heartbeat back under control. I was vaguely aware of doors opening and shutting all around me. As my scream's echo faded away and the darkness at the edge of my vision began to clear, I also could hear anxious voices. I stood up and gave the corpse a curious look.

I immediately recognized her. There was a spreading pool of blood beneath her head, and her gray-streaked reddish braids were floating in it. Given the glassy appearance of her wide-open, staring eyes, she was clearly dead with no chance of resuscitation. I'd apparently dropped my cell phone when I screamed, so I reached for it on the table and noticed that my hand was shaking. *Get a grip, dear. A corpse just landed at your feet—no one would expect you to be completely calm under these circumstances,* I said to myself as I deleted the strongly worded text I'd been writing Jerry and pulled up the phone keypad. I took a few deep breaths as I punched in 9-1-1. When a bored-sounding woman answered, I patiently explained what had happened and suggested she send an ambulance and the police. I ended the call and sat back down heavily in the metal chair. People started materializing in the various entryways to the courtyard and the staircase landings in the main building, gasping when they realized what they were looking at.

Jerry had told me that this massive building on Toulouse Street had once been a single-family dwelling. The back building and the wing dividing the two courtyards and connecting the back building to the front had been slave quarters. The Maison Maintenon had been converted sometime in the last thirty years or so into a boutique hotel. It was actually kind of hard to fathom that this enormous brick mansion had housed only one family. They must have been rolling in cash when they built the place back in the 1870s. The Maintenon family and their fortune were long gone—I think they died out during the First World War. I didn't know who currently owned the place, but it was one of the few privately owned hotels remaining in the French Quarter, as chains had taken over the majority of them. The slave quarters were now deluxe luxury suites with kitchenettes and large living rooms. Since there was no gallery on the third floor of the slave quarters, I assumed the second-floor suites were two-story lofts. What had been the main house was four stories high, and I had no idea how many rooms there were for rent. As with many old homes in southeastern Louisiana, the staircase and hallways on the upper floors of the main building were open air from this side, and even more people were coming to the railings at the end of those halls to look down at the grisly scene. The ice machine in the dark passage into the jungle-like courtyard on the other side rumbled as it created another load of ice, and I heard the cockatoo that lived in a gigantic bamboo cage hanging from an ancient live oak branch over there squawk rather loudly.

I shoved my phone back into my shoulder bag and wished I had a glass of bourbon or wine or something—*anything*—alcoholic, and cursed myself for leaving my flask back in my own room before heading over, thinking I wouldn't need it. I drummed my fingers on the tabletop, trying not to look back at the corpse.

That resolve lasted about twenty seconds, and I shook my head.

Because I *recognized* her—but I barely knew her.

Yesterday I wouldn't have known her from Adam.

I had met her earlier in the day at the airport in Atlanta—a hellhole if there ever was one. As I made my way through the crowds in the enormous concourses to the gate for my connecting flight to New Orleans, I couldn't help but wonder what Dante would have made of it. *He certainly would have made it one of the outer circles of hell,* I thought as I bought an overpriced bottle of water from a bored cashier in a convenience store and took a sip before venturing back out into the crowds. What I really needed was coffee, but I'd had several cups of airline coffee on the flight down and my stomach felt like sulfuric acid was trying to eat through the lining despite the antacids I'd been gulping down. I really needed to eat something, but the lines at every place I'd seen were so long and the connection so tight I was afraid to risk it.

I had to take one of those horrible underground trains to another concourse, where I gratefully sat down in the waiting area for Delta flight 3724. I quickly checked my phone for emails—and finding none that couldn't wait, retrieved the book I was reading out of my bag. I was lost in Megan Abbott's dark world of high school cheerleading, sipping at my water bottle and peacefully minding my own business when someone plopped down so heavily in the seat next to me that I dropped my book, promptly losing my place. I did manage to hang on to the bottle of water. Irritated, I gave her a stern look.

"Oh, terribly sorry, did I make you drop that?" she said in a squeaky high-pitched voice that seemed more appropriate for a twelve-year-old than the rather large older woman squeezed into the seat next to mine. She also didn't sound in the least bit sorry. She had a British accent, but from an area of the country I couldn't quite place. It definitely wasn't London, and she didn't sound posh—she definitely hadn't been to Oxford or

Cambridge. If I had to go out on a limb I would have said it was one of the northern counties. When I'd been in London for a year in college I'd dated a girl named Moira from Yorkshire, and there were definite similarities in this woman's accent to Moira's.

The woman blinked her watery, bloodshot blue eyes at me a few times, her enormous smile exposing yellowed, crooked teeth, and I could smell her stale breath.

I leaned forward and picked up my book. *Be polite. Remember, you don't know this woman and she didn't make you do it on purpose.* "No problem," I replied, making my voice neutral yet pleasant and forcing a smile. "No harm done, really." I started flipping through the pages to find my lost place.

"This is my first time in the States, you know," she said, reaching into the huge canvas shoulder bag she'd plopped down in the seat on the other side of her and pulling out a bag of barbecue-flavored pork rinds. "I'm so bloody excited, I really am, but all I've seen so far is the inside of this bloody airport and of course the terribly rude people at your customs and I can't say I much care for it so far." She used her grayish, crooked front teeth to tear the bag open and grabbed a fistful of the pork rinds, which she shoved into her mouth, dusting the front of her polyester print blouse with crumbs.

Don't engage, do not engage, I told myself as I found my place and started reading again, pointedly ignoring her.

I might have known she wasn't the type to take the hint.

She hadn't even finished chewing the abominable pork rinds before she started speaking again, crumbs flying out in every direction with each syllable. "I suppose New Orleans'll be more of the same." She sniffed disdainfully, rustling the bag as she dug out another handful of fried pig skin. "Americans really like having everything new and the same, don't you? I simply don't understand it. In England we appreciate history and character, you know. We don't simply bulldoze over everything and try to make it all the same." She chortled. "Can you imagine?"

Okay, that's it. I marked the page with my bookmark and closed the book with a decisive snap. "Actually, New Orleans is nothing like Atlanta, and even Atlanta isn't like its airport—after all, you can't really judge London if all you've seen is Heathrow, can you?" I said slowly, counting to ten in my head as I turned my head to look at her, using my patented I'm-your-teacher-don't-fuck-with-me glare.

She goggled at me again with her small, watery blue eyes as she shoved another handful of pork rinds into her mouth. She had a moon face, with several extra chins hanging underneath. Her skin was incredibly pale—the kind that can get a nasty sunburn just by stepping out into direct sunlight. Her wispy, coppery hair was shot through with gray and pulled back into a loose bun at the base of her neck. Stray strands floated about in the air around her head. Her nose was broad and flat, with a turned-up tip that unfortunately gave it a rather snout-like look. The polyester orange-and-brown geometric patterned blouse she was wearing had flounces at the neck and all the way down the front. The blouse was an unfortunate choice, as it made her look larger.

Her stomach was so large she was forced to sit with her brown stretch-panted legs spread apart. The blouse was short-sleeved, and her large, flabby upper arms jiggled every time she moved. There was also a slightly sour smell underneath the cloying lavender scent she'd drenched herself in, a combination of sweat and body odor. On her right wrist she was wearing a gold bracelet with what appeared to be *Midnight* character charms hanging from the links.

Oh dear God, she's one of those, I thought with a slight recoil.

Midnight was a series of books, extremely popular with teenage girls (and some older women), that had sold millions upon millions of copies since the first one was released around the turn of the century. It was about a pair of twins—one boy, one girl—who find out, upon reaching puberty, that they are actually descended from a long line of witches when a mage shows up at the home of their (naturally quite abusive) foster parents. They are whisked away from their horrible home life to a training camp for supernatural teens, and of course, both become involved in turgid romances with classmates. The girl, Megara, apparently had the power to make every male who came into contact with her fall madly in love with her, whether it was a ghost, a vampire, a werewolf, a shifter, a faerie—pretty much if it had a pulse and a penis, it fell madly in love with Megara. The young girls who were fans of the books became completely devoted to them, even choosing sides (or "teams," as they preferred to be called) about who Megara should spend all of eternity with.

Her unfortunate twin brother, Orion, didn't quite inspire the passion Megara did in the fans, at least not that I was aware of—but I didn't follow the phenomenon that closely. It was hard to not get some knowledge by osmosis, though—the *Midnight* books and the films based on them were everywhere. The fans called themselves "Twelvers" (as in "twelve midnight") and would line up at bookstores the night before the latest edition was going to be released. The books, films, and merchandise were a billion-dollar industry, and the not-particularly-talented author was so filthy rich she annually made the *Forbes* list of wealthiest Americans.

I'd tried to read the first one but it was so poorly written, the characters so derivative and cardboard that not only did I throw it away unfinished, I buried it in the bottom of a trash bag. I didn't want anyone seeing it in my garbage and knowing that I'd actually wasted fourteen dollars on that crap.

The woman sitting beside me tilted her head back and emptied the debris left inside the bag into her mouth, then smiled at me.

Pork rind dust covered her teeth.

"So, what brings you to New Orleans?" I asked, knowing I'd hate myself in a moment for continuing the conversation rather than getting up and moving to another seat, but I was actually curious.

She beamed proudly at me before rummaging in her bag again. She pulled out a book and shoved it at me. "I'm going to Angels and Demons, the gay writers' conference."

Given no real choice, I took the book from her as my heart sank. I was also going to Angels and Demons. *Is she a lesbian?* I wondered, turning my attention from her to the book. It was an oversized trade paperback, with a publisher's logo I didn't recognize. I looked at the front cover. Two men—one with blond hair, the other with dark—were embracing, their lips pursed as they were clearly about to kiss. Their ruffled shirts were open, exposing broad, hairless, muscular chests with enormous nipples. They were wearing tight breeches and knee-high boots. In Gothic script across the top was the title: *THE KING'S SWORD.* At the bottom was a name in the same script: ANTINOUS RENAULT.

Antinous Renault? Seriously?

"*The King's Sword*," I replied slowly, trying to wrap my mind around it. "A gay historical?"

"Yes, indeed, how clever you are! It's indeed a gay historical romance." She bobbed her head up and down. "The market's really, really untapped," she said seriously. "Since Mary Renault died, there haven't been many gay historicals, you know. And with m/m becoming such a huge genre—it really *is* the big new thing in publishing—I'm very proud to carry the banner for gay historicals." She exhaled, giving me a strong whiff of sour breath not completely masked by the smell of pork rinds.

"Antinous," I said, half to myself as I turned the book over. On the back, directly in the center of the plot's description, was a thumbprint in crusted chocolate.

Well, I *assumed* it was chocolate.

"Antinous was the Roman Emperor Hadrian's lover," she went on breathlessly, an idyllic, almost orgasmic look on her face. "He was the most beautiful man in the world—"

I cut her off, annoyed. "I'm well aware of who Antinous was, thank you very much. I have a degree in classical history. My specialty was the Roman Empire." Nothing irritates me more than someone assuming I'm stupid, which happens all the damned time.

It's the blond hair, blue eyes, and what used to be called a peaches-and-cream complexion. If I had a dollar for every time someone assumed I was a dumb blonde I'd never have to work another day in my life.

Okay, my specialty had actually been the Plantagenets, but I'd studied the Roman Empire and knew who Antinous was.

I narrowed my eyes.

The woman was, however, completely oblivious to the fact she'd given offense. Her smile never wavered even for a moment. She tilted her head slightly to one side in a birdlike way and went on, "And of course I took Renault to honor Mary Renault, because she really was such a trailblazer and one of the biggest inspirations for my work." She sighed blissfully. "Reading *The Persian Boy* literally changed my life. I'd never thought about writing about yummy gay men before that."

Mary Renault is probably rolling in her grave, I thought, *and she really did not just describe gay men as yummy, did she?*

I hate when people use food terms to describe people. I bit my tongue to keep from asking how many gay men she had actually tasted.

"Have you read it? It's so wonderful."

"Yes." I stopped myself from adding that I hardly considered *The Persian Boy,* which opened with a rather graphic castration scene, a "gay romance novel." But as I looked at her, my irritation started to fade and I began to feel sorry for her. She really was rather unfortunate looking.

And clearly, the irony of her use of Antinous as a pseudonym was apparently lost on her. No one ever would use the words "the most beautiful creature on earth" to describe her, the poor dear.

I turned my attention back to the book in my hand and read the blurb on the back cover. It was set during the Scots uprising in favor of Bonnie Prince Charlie in the eighteenth century, when the overthrown Stuarts made their final attempt to regain the British throne and oust the German House of Hanover. I smiled to myself—there really *was* nothing quite so romantic as a lost cause. According to the text, the romantic conflict in the book came from the fact that one of the lovers was in the royal army while the other supported Bonnie Prince Charlie. *A bit far-fetched,* I thought, *but then again, aren't all romance novels kind of far-fetched?*

God knows I'd written some pretty far-fetched lesbian romances.

Farther down on the back cover there was an author photo of an extraordinarily handsome young man next to the author bio. I looked up at her and pointedly back down to the author photo, then back again.

She chortled and rolled her eyes. "Yes, you've noticed the author photo. No, that's not me, obviously." She threw back her head and brayed loudly with laughter for a few moments. She wiped at her eyes and sighed. "When I was first getting started, you know, there was a mindset that gay men wouldn't read books by straight women, which of course is completely absurd on its face—after all, they read Mary Renault and Patricia Nell Warren, don't they?"

I refrained from pointing out Renault and Warren were both lesbians.

"But my publisher *insisted* on using a male model for my author photos and insisted on pretending I was a man." She rolled her eyes theatrically. "Like gay men are sexist! It really is completely absurd."

I've known any number of sexist gay men, I thought, but didn't say it out loud. But there was some truth to that—men have traditionally *always* ignored books by women and denigrated women authors. It was an endless struggle for women authors, requiring eternal vigilance, and I felt myself warming to her a little more. She might be lacking in social graces, but like me, she was also a woman author struggling against sexism in the publishing world.

I started to pass the book back to her with a slight

smile. "So, you write gay historical romances? That must be really difficult to research, given the way queers have been systematically erased from history."

She chortled again, reaching into her bag and pulling out a bottle of Mountain Dew. She took a big swig, recapped it, and put it back in her bag. "Oh, it's not that hard. I do it all online. Everything's on the Internet, you know. I don't know *how* people did research before! *Imagine* having to spend all that time in a library! Or sorting through books to find that one little nugget of information you need!"

Oh my God.

I bit my lower lip to stop from saying something I might regret. It's been a problem ever since I was a child—I tend to blurt things out that are probably best left unsaid. But the very idea of writing historical novels while only doing research over the web was so patently wrong and absurd that I wanted to shake some sense into her.

The historian in me wanted to slap her stupid face.

Somehow I managed to instead nod politely. "Yes, libraries are horrible places, aren't they? All that *dust.*"

I wasn't surprised that my sarcasm was completely lost on her. "Yes, that's it exactly! Oh, it's so lovely to meet someone who understands!" She leaned in toward me, and I involuntarily moved away from her. "I mean, why waste the petrol and all that time when everything's available online? You can find out everything you need in the comfort of your own home!"

Oh, I understand all right. You're a hack. I kept my smile frozen in place as I replied, "Yes, I'm certain Mary Renault would conduct her research online if she were alive today."

And again, she took my statement at face value. Her head bobbed up and down theatrically. She elbowed me, chortling a bit. "Yes, you're absolutely right, of course! Imagine how much more work she could have done had she not been limited by the almost *primitive* technology she had to work with! Imagine if she could have researched at home, or written on a computer rather than a typewriter!" She took the book from me and pulled out a grimy-looking Sharpie from her bag. "I'll let you keep this." She beamed at me. "Just let me sign it for you."

I'd rather have cholera, I thought, deciding that I'd be polite and take it—and throw it away at the first opportunity.

She scribbled away on the title page. "It's my fifth novel, and critics have simply *raved* about my work—five stars on Amazon and Goodreads, and all the important gay romance blogs."

All the important gay romance blogs?

"I'm writing another now—it's more of a romantic suspense novel, set in the nineteenth century, where a young man comes to a gloomy manor to tutor the master's son..."

As she rambled on in quite exhaustive detail, I let my own mind wander a bit. I didn't need to pay a lot of attention—the plot she was telling me sounded like a rip-off of both Victoria Holt's *The King of the Castle* and *Jane Eyre*, with a bit of *The Castle of Otranto* added in for good measure. The primary difference from those classics, of course, was that this woman's version had only gay male characters and, apparently, a lot of gay sex scenes.

Besides, it was patently obvious that all she needed from me was an occasional grunt or nod anyway.

And I was extremely tired. I'd had to get up at four in the morning and drive two hours south to Albany to catch my absurdly early flight to Atlanta, and my efforts to secure an upgrade to first class on that flight had proven to be in vain. I'd wound up stuck in the back of the plane, and I just can't sleep in the coach cabin. I'd drunk enough coffee to float an ocean liner, but rather than waking me up it simply made me nauseous as well as tired and sleepy. All I wanted to do was curl up somewhere and go to sleep, and I stifled a yawn as she prattled on.

This was my last trip back to Louisiana before my gig as writer-in-residence at Wilbourne College in upstate New York finally wound down. It had been a great gig—the kind that were becoming fewer and farther between these days with cutbacks happening in education on every level. But Wilbourne College was an old private women's college, founded in the mid-nineteenth century for proper young ladies from good families. The tuition was ridiculous, but the school's reputation for providing an excellent education had only grown over time, and it had the kind of endowment the University of Louisiana at Rouen, where I was tenured, wouldn't have the nerve to dream of having. I hadn't even had to think twice when the chancellor of Wilbourne had called with the offer. The gig was too good to pass up—a ridiculous salary, I only had to teach one graduate-level writing class, and it came with a furnished one-bedroom cottage a short walk from the campus that was absolutely adorable—cozy, warm, and comfortable in the brutal winter. I flew back down to Louisiana every other weekend, to check on my house and pay my bills. Unfortunately, I wouldn't have time on this trip to get over to my house in Rouen, the small college town about an hour northwest of New Orleans where I lived, but it didn't matter—I'd be coming home for good soon enough. All I had left to do at Wilbourne was return my students' last short stories to them, file my final grades, pack up my office and the little house, and ship everything back down here. I already had my plane ticket home purchased. It would, I reflected, be nice to be back home. Even though I loved it at Wilbourne, Louisiana was *home*.

Honestly, the timing of this trip to New Orleans was bad for me. I'd been avoiding writers' conferences, too, over the last few years. If you've done one, you've done them all, really.

But when my old friend Jerry asked me to teach a master class and do some panels at the annual Angels and Demons LGBT Literary Festival, being held in New Orleans for the first time in its twelve-year history, I couldn't say no, even though I'd done a pretty good job of avoiding New Orleans as much as possible in the last ten years.

You'll be there for four days, and she doesn't know you as Winter Lovelace, I reminded myself. *Nobody in New Orleans knows you as Winter Lovelace.*

That was the beauty of using a pseudonym—all the publicity materials for the conference listed me as Winter Lovelace rather than my real name, Tracy Norris.

Tracy Norris was a professor of English at the University of Louisiana-Rouen who also wrote critically acclaimed, award-winning crime novels about a kick-ass Louisiana female private eye named Laura Lassiter. Winter Lovelace, on the other hand, wrote torrid lesbian romances with lots of graphic, hot sex scenes.

And only my agent, and a handful of others who'd put the clues together, knew the two writers were actually the same woman.

It wasn't that I was ashamed of the romances. I had copies of them proudly on the bookshelf in my office on campus at Wilbourne just as I did in my office at ULR, and while I didn't use the same author photo as Winter that I did as Tracy, anyone looking at the pictures side by side would think they were either of the same person or of two women who looked so much alike they could be twins. I also wasn't ashamed of being a lesbian. I've been out since I was in high school—at Sacred Heart Academy for Girls on St. Charles Avenue in New Orleans, no less.

No, when I decided to try my hand at writing a lesbian romance, my agent, Mabel Clegg, told me she could sell it to a small lesbian press—but recommended I use a pseudonym to differentiate it from the crime novels.

"The lesbian romances won't sell as well as the crime books, and you don't want the low sales for one to affect the others," Mabel had insisted. "Trust me, it happens. We need to protect the Tracy Norris brand—we've worked too hard building it up over the years to wreck it now."

I hated being referred to as a brand—like I'm dishwashing liquid or laundry soap or something—but I always listened to Mabel, even if it bothered my lesbian sensibilities.

I didn't like using the pseudonym, but I'd gotten used to it over the years. Mabel was a great agent—the editor of the Laura series once told me that Mabel would scare a shark— and she did know the business inside and out. She'd never once steered me wrong, and it is a foolish author who ignores their agent's advice.

And one thing I am not is a fool.

I was just two months past my deadline for my next Laura Lassiter novel.

In fact, I reminded myself, *you should be working on it here while you wait to get on the plane.*

I realized with a start that Antinous Renault had apparently finished talking by asking me a question and was waiting for me to answer her.

"I'm sorry." I gave her a guilty smile. "I completely forgot what you asked."

She twittered and leaned toward me. "It's all right, dearie, he is good-looking, isn't he?" She smacked her lips like she was about to eat something delicious. "Gay men are so yummy, aren't they?"

Startled and more than a little repulsed, I turned my head to see the young man she was looking at. I wasn't sure he was gay—it's getting harder and harder to tell anymore, what with young straight men embracing the use of hair and skin products and paying more attention to their clothes and spending hours in the gym—but he was good-looking, if you liked men.

Which...

I turned and looked at Antinous again. She was staring at the young man with her mouth and eyes wide open. She licked her lips and nudged me with her elbow again, chortling. "There's nothing hotter than two men together, is there?" She was rubbing her knees with her hands as she said it. "I swear, I don't know why anyone would write anything besides m/m."

"What's m/m?"

She patted my leg with one of her small hands, which were covered with red splotches and looked almost grotesque given how large her forearms were. Her nails were bitten to the quick, yet still managed to look dirty. "Male-male, of course. It's the hottest new trend in publishing."

"I've never heard of it." I frowned. "Why isn't it just called gay?"

She was nodding again. "It's a very hot trend," she went on. "You know, women writing male romances."

I shook my head again. "I'm sorry, I don't understand."

She patted my leg again in that patronizing way that made

me want to slap her. "It started out as straight women writing for other straight women—*Queer as Folk* fanfic, mostly, but then it expanded to other fandoms. I myself came to it from *Midnight* fandom." She smacked her lips in a rather revolting way. "I mostly wrote Ptolemy/Orion romance."

What? I can't have heard that right. If I remember what little of the book I read, Ptolemy was a centuries-old mage. I gaped at her. "But…Orion was a kid."

"Oh, you bloody Americans and your prudish age of consent! In the UK it's sixteen, so of course I made Orion sixteen in my stories!" She slapped my leg and chortled again. "But when I found out there was this market out there for original gay romances, and given my interest in history, well, writing gay historical romances simply made the most sense."

"So you're straight?"

"My sexuality is fluid." She snorted rather loftily, as though I were not sophisticated enough to understand. "I mean, I find women incredibly attractive but getting one into bed, well, they're just so much work! I just don't have the patience for that." She shook her head, her jowls swinging, and snorted again. "I'm much too lazy to work that hard, you know? I thought I might be transgendered for a while, but no, I'm all woman and proud of it. I'm fairly certain I'm just bisexual." She rummaged in her bag again and pulled out another bag of pork rinds. "Besides, I don't really leave my house that much anymore. I just stay home and take care of my cats and write and communicate with my fans on social media." She leaned in closer. "And I get literally *thousands* of emails from gay men who love and appreciate my work."

Thousands?

"And all of us who write m/m, you know, we're all terribly committed to the cause."

I shook my head. "The cause?"

"Gay equality, of course." She virtuously pressed a splotchy hand to her massive chest. "Why, just last year I co-edited an anthology to raise money for gay equality. We raised *over* a thousand dollars! The book was an enormous success!" She nudged me with her elbow again. "If only one of my books sold as well as the anthology!"

I was about to point out that if the anthology had only made a thousand dollars and sold better than her novels, then she couldn't possibly have thousands of fans, when the gate agent called me up to the counter. I was delighted to be handed an upgrade to first class, and as they started boarding the first-class cabin at that moment, I didn't speak to Antinous again.

In fact, I'd pretty much forgotten about her until her body landed a few feet away from me.

I finished giving information to the 911 operator just as I saw Jerry Channing running across the courtyard toward me.

CHAPTER TWO

"Well, that was a rather unpleasant start for the weekend," I commented as I unfolded my napkin and draped it across my lap.

"Yes, welcome home," Jerry Channing replied with a theatrical roll of his eyes. "So glad you could make it down."

We were seated at Muriel's on the Square, a rather lovely restaurant on the corner of St. Ann and Chartres, just across from Jackson Square. The hostess had seated us at a table in the window on the Chartres Street side of the building. The restaurant was almost empty and fairly quiet, which was nice. It was just after nine. They closed at ten, so I didn't feel so bad about getting there so late. I'd waited tables when I was a college student, so I knew far too well how much it sucked to have customers come in right before closing. I tried not to ever do it, except in the case of a dire food emergency. This definitely qualified as one. I was so hungry I would have eaten pretty much anything put in front of me. I'd had a bagel with my coffee at the airport in Albany, and I'd barely had time to get checked into my hotel and unpack before heading over to the Maison Maintenon to meet Jerry for dinner.

The little foil-wrapped chocolates Housekeeping had left on my pillow hadn't done the trick.

And then, of course, there was the little matter of having to deal with the police after Antinous Renault's untimely death.

One thing I didn't miss in the ten years since I'd moved across the lake to Rouen was dealing with the New Orleans Police Department. At first, as the EMTs dealt with the obviously dead body, I'd been questioned by an extremely polite and friendly young woman of color who went out of her way to make me comfortable. I'd even made a mental note to write her sergeant a commendation letter for her professionalism. Had it ended there, all would have been well.

Unfortunately, the detective in charge of the investigation was an all-too-typical misogynist asshole by the name of Al Randisi, and he insisted on interviewing me himself. He was balding, with a really ridiculous-looking light-brown comb-over that was the height of self-delusion. He was tall, most likely one of those idiots who'd been a big-deal jock in high school—the Big Man on Campus type that had no idea how much everyone really hated him, the type that never got over the unearned sense of entitlement and believed that every woman he met wanted him on sight.

He was a stereotype straight out of Central Casting. "Get me a misogynist asshole cop type!"

To be fair, it was entirely possible that Al Randisi might have been a good-looking man in high school and maybe even well into his twenties...but years of not taking care of himself had taken their toll. He looked like he'd been on a steady diet of Pabst Blue Ribbon and fried everything for about twenty years.

He had wide shoulders and a beer gut that hung almost painfully over his too-tight belt. He had one of those unfortunate bodies with a low, narrow waist and slender legs so he rather looked like Humpty Dumpty sitting on the wall. His yellow-and-blue paisley tie had several stains so old they probably predated Katrina, and it wasn't knotted correctly. I could see his white undershirt through his pale blue shirt, but he'd still managed to sweat through both layers at the armpits. He wore a pair of blue polyester pants and cheap black shoes and stank of cigarette smoke and sweat and a cheap men's cologne bought at a drugstore.

He was also a patronizing asshole who kept calling me "little lady," which made me want to grab the gun out of his shoulder holster and put a bullet in the center of his forehead.

I had told him my story I don't know how many times before he finally decided he'd heard it enough and dismissed me with a condescending wave of his hand.

The fact that I somehow managed to remain calm and not give him the tongue-lashing he deserved should qualify me for the Nobel Peace Prize.

I was exhausted, hungry, and desperately in need of a long, relaxing soak in a tub.

"I knew there was a reason I shouldn't come this weekend. You really, really owe me one now," I said darkly as I opened my menu. "Although I'd imagine this is going to be a nightmare for you." I didn't even try to fake sympathy. I was too tired and hungry.

"No, not really, it doesn't have anything to do with the conference," Jerry replied, taking a sip from his sweating glass of ice water. "Didn't you think it was weird, though, the way the police were all over it? I mean, obviously it was an accident, right? She fell over the railing. Probably just lost her balance and went over and *splat*." He shrugged. "Sure, it's a tragedy, but hardly worthy of a full police investigation."

"It wasn't an accidental fall. For one thing, she didn't fall far enough to really kill herself. Broken some bones, certainly, but it was what? Maybe ten feet? She would have had to land on her head for it to have killed her." I closed my eyes and tried to remember yet another time how it happened. "Jerry, she landed pretty much flat on her back. If you fall over a railing, it's not likely you'd land flat on your back like that." I shook my head. "She didn't scream or cry out, either—how likely is that? You don't fall like that without screaming." My mind was whirring along merrily. "In fact, if someone shoved her over, she would have screamed."

So she had to already be dead when she went over the railing.

"So, your professional opinion is murder?" He arched an eyebrow at me. "Are you going to play Jessica Fletcher this weekend?"

"I'm not a professional investigator, so it's not my *professional* opinion."

His eyes glinted and he gave me his trademark wicked smile. "But you *are* a professional crime writer, and you research crimes and police procedures, don't you? And really, you had a body practically land in your lap! How can you pass this up?"

"I'll gladly leave the investigating to the cops," I replied with a theatrical eye roll and shuddered. "I have no interest in real-life crime, except from a very safe distance, thank you very much."

"Okay, so let's pretend this was one of your books," he went on smoothly. "And Laura Lassiter is on the case." He winked. "And she always gets her man, doesn't she?"

I couldn't help it, I had to laugh. Reviewers and readers always complained about Laura's lack of a successful love life. I did have a tendency to kill off pretty much every man romantically involved with her—Jerry wickedly once called her "the fuck of death," and it made me laugh. *Always getting her man* was a variation of the same theme, especially because in two of the books her lovers turned out to be the killers and she wound up shooting them in self-defense in the end after figuring it out.

"If Laura was on the case," I said, wiping the tears out of my eyes and feeling kind of bad for laughing about someone's death, "of course it would be murder, and everyone at the conference would have a motive for killing her."

"Well, if you think someone shoved her over that railing, there had to be at least two of them," he replied with a bitchy smirk. "It's not like she was a delicate flower."

"Still the mean one," I replied with a faint smile and a slight shake of my head. It was another running gag between us—that I'm the nice one and he's the mean one.

"You just say that because I'll say out loud what you're thinking."

In response, I laughed and shook my head. He really was incorrigible. I've known him for over twenty years, and he has always been able to make me laugh. Jerry has an absolutely wicked sense of humor—bitchy and snarky, but he really has a big heart and would give anyone the shirt off his back.

Then again, he'll jump at any excuse to take his shirt off.

We'd first met when we were both students at the University of New Orleans. We both took the same creative writing class taught by a ridiculously pompous fool who knew next to nothing about writing. We didn't know that at the time we took the class, of course—well, the pompous part was apparent on Day One. The rest we figured out over the course of the semester—laughing about him later in Jerry's apartment on Burgundy Street in the Quarter while drinking horrible cheap wine and smoking really good pot.

When I walked into the classroom on the first day of the fall semester of my sophomore year, I felt ready to collapse from the heat. August is unpleasant everywhere in Louisiana, but the University of New Orleans campus is right on the lakefront, and the high protective levee at the very edge of campus shielded it not only from rising water but from any refreshing breezes that might be blowing in from the water. Stepping out of the air-conditioned buildings was like climbing into an oven and slamming the door behind you. I was worried I was going to be late—moving through the horribly hot thick air was miserable and my Joan Jett T-shirt was soaked through by the time I was able to get inside again. But when I reached the classroom I could see there was no teacher in the front of the room. I stood in the doorway and looked around. There were about twenty students in the room, with an empty desk next to what appeared to be the only gay guy in the room.

He might not be gay, I'd chastised myself as I slid into the desk and smiled at him, *but he is definitely setting off my gaydar.*

When I was a student, no straight guy would even *consider* shaving his legs or waxing his armpits or watching his diet so he could have a six-pack. Anytime you saw a guy who was well-groomed with smooth legs and armpits in those days, you could be 99.99% certain he was gay. And this guy had no body hair on any of the skin he had exposed—which was quite a bit. So he was either gay or hadn't hit puberty yet—which was hardly likely.

He was slouched so far down in his chair his ass was barely on the edge of the seat, and his arms were crossed. He was wearing a black muscle T-shirt that was probably a size too small, given the way it stretched across his muscular torso and strained at the seams. He was wearing tight white cut-off Daisy Dukes (another sign—straight boys were already wearing shorts down to their knees by then), and his long, tanned hairless legs were stretched out under his desk and crossed at the ankles. Wisps of curly, bluish-black hair hung out from underneath the Saints baseball cap perched backward on top of his head, and black Ray-Ban sunglasses hid his eyes. He turned his head slightly and gave me a bit of a nod before turning back to stare at the front of the room as a balding white-haired man in corduroy slacks and a maroon-and-yellow-striped button-down shirt strolled in and placed a briefcase on the table in the front of the room. The few students who were talking to each other fell silent, and he gave us what was supposed to be a "serious professor" look that actually made him look constipated. He picked up a piece of chalk and wrote *Dr. Dixon* in big, sloping letters across the green board before turning around and smiling at us.

I liked the original constipated look better. The smile was kind of creepy, like there were teenage boys buried in quick-lime in his backyard.

He cleared his throat. "Henry James is the greatest author to ever string a sentence together." He spent the rest of the hour explaining to us, in great detail, precisely why Henry James was the greatest author of all time, and that he hoped that we would all learn in his class to not only appreciate the genius of Henry James, but to emulate him in our writing styles. He also urged us to read everything of James's we could, and actually assigned us to read a short story called "The Beast in the Jungle."

I'd read it in high school and absolutely hated it.

The class couldn't end soon enough. I gathered my things and escaped to the student union, where I grabbed a can of Diet Coke and sat down in a corner. I'd always wanted to be a writer—my earliest memories were of me curled up somewhere reading a book. I'd read the entire Nancy Drew and Trixie Belden series by the time I was ten, when I moved on to Agatha Christie. I couldn't remember a time when I didn't want to write books. I wrote my first story, a Nancy Drew rip-off called *Tiffany Lane and the Secret of Hartwood Manor,* when I was eight—I actually still had it in my files at home. My favorite stores had always been bookstores, and while other girls my age were buying dolls and teen magazines, I was buying books. The only place I loved more than a bookstore was a library, and I especially loved the Latter Library on St. Charles Avenue. Every Saturday morning for years I caught the streetcar at Felicity Street and rode it uptown, getting off at Soniat Street and lugging the books I was returning in a backpack through the front doors of the beautiful old mansion converted into a library. My parents loved that I was a reader—my older brother was a painter and had never had much interest in reading.

My teachers at the Academy of the Sacred Heart encouraged me in my dreams. I wrote for the school newspaper, and in my spare time when I wasn't studying I was busy writing stories in my spiral notebooks in pencil—but by then I was well aware that I was more interested in other girls than in boys, so I wrote love stories where two girls fell in love. Usually my heroine was a bookish girl who got straight As, and the girl who fell in love with her was the incredibly beautiful and immensely popular captain of the field hockey/basketball/softball/volleyball teams. I never showed those stories to anyone, of course—the stories I turned in for my creative writing classes were heteronormative. Everyone at Sacred Heart knew I was a lesbian—I'd proudly come out at fourteen, with my parents' full support—but as long as I didn't talk about it, no one seemed to care. I just kept to myself, did my homework, read books, and wrote my stories.

So, that day in the Student Union, I pulled a spiral notebook out of my backpack and opened it to the current story I was writing—about a private eye named Laura. Over the summer, after high school graduation, I'd discovered Sue Grafton and Sara Paretsky and Marcia Muller, and I wanted to be just like them, writing about strong, independent women who didn't take any shit from men and solved crimes. I looked at where I'd left off, thought for a moment, and started scribbling hurriedly in pencil again.

A deep voice said from behind me, "Henry James is without question the most *constipated* writer in the history of the English language."

Startled, I dropped my pencil as the guy in the black muscle shirt and white Daisy Dukes sat down on the other side of the table from me. He took off his sunglasses, revealing two large, expressive brown eyes that were twinkling at me. He was grinning, and two deep dimples pierced his cheeks. "Jerry Channing," he said, popping the top of his own Coke can. "And you are?"

"Tracy Norris." I smiled back at him. "And I fucking *hate* Henry James."

"You a lesbian?"

"Yeah," I replied. "You gay?"

His grin got wider. "Yup."

It turned out Jerry was from upstate Mississippi, some "little buttfuck town in the middle of no place where everyone's been marrying their cousins since Indian days" (his words, not mine) and his parents had thrown him out when he was seventeen after catching him with the preacher's son ("Yes," he intoned seriously, "I was deflowered by the son of a preacher man"), and he'd hitchhiked his way to New Orleans. He was vague about the next couple of years and I didn't press him on it—I suspected he'd been hustling—but now he was working as a personal trainer and moonlighted sometimes as a stripper. He'd gotten his GED and saved his money till he was finally able to swing the tuition at UNO. "And," he winked at me, "I'm going to be the most famous fucking faggot in this country so I can rub my parents' faces in it."

I couldn't help it, I started laughing. When I was able to get control of myself again, I asked, "How are you going to get famous?"

"Writing."

I smiled back at him. "Me, too!"

And thus a beautiful friendship was born.

In fact, our friendship was the longest relationship either of us had ever had.

I'm not sure I like what that says about me.

"Anyway, it's nice to have you back in the city," he said with a smile, reaching over and touching my hand lightly, pulling me back to the present. "I hate not seeing you all the time. Why don't you move back?"

I shook my head. "I like living on the north shore, Jerry. Rouen suits me fine. And I really enjoy our email exchanges." Jerry was more of a night person—I always had an eight a.m. class to teach and had gotten into the habit of getting up around six every morning. Before getting ready to go to work, I spent an hour with my coffee, yogurt, and fresh fruit answering the fifty or so emails he'd sent me around one in the morning. We agreed on almost everything, from politics to television to books.

The only thing we didn't agree about was my move to Rouen ten years earlier. He was constantly trying to talk me into moving back to the south shore.

I took another drink of my water and decided to have the double-cut pork chop and pain perdu for dessert, rationalizing to myself that since I was in New Orleans it would be *wrong* to eat healthy.

"I suppose tomorrow night at the opening reception we're going to have to do a moment of silence or something in the bitch's honor," Jerry went on as he glanced at his menu with a sigh. His phone vibrated, and he looked at the screen with a scowl. "I wish I had a dollar for every text I've gotten asking if I'm canceling the weekend. Why, yes, let's write the whole weekend off because that stupid British bitch fell off a balcony—excuse me, was *pushed* off a balcony." He shook his head. "I'm just sorry you had to see it happen." He reached across the table and patted my hand. "Are you sure you're doing okay?"

I gave him a withering look. "I'm not a shrinking violet, Jerry. I've seen worse than that when I was in the Peace Corps." I repressed a shudder at the memory of Ethiopia during the worst of the famine years. "Anyway, it was just an odd coincidence that I met her at the airport in Atlanta, I suppose."

He arched an eyebrow up. "You met her?"

I nodded. "We were on the same connecting flight."

"I know you're not supposed to speak ill of the dead, but

she was a *bitch,*" Jerry hissed before giving our waitress a big smile and ordering a bottle of Barolo wine. After she went away, he smiled at me. "Sorry to order for you, but I figured you'd want a nice glass of Barolo. You know, to help calm your nerves."

"One can never go wrong with a fine wine, you know." I smiled back at him. "It frightens me how well you know me."

"If only you were a man."

"If only you were a woman," I countered as the waitress filled our glasses and took our orders.

Once she was gone, Jerry raised his wineglass. "If only Dr. Dixon could see us now."

I grinned wickedly back at him as I clinked my glass against his. Dear old Dr. Dixon *hated* both Jerry's and my writing. After our first stories were turned in, he required all of us students to make an appointment for a "conference" on our work. Jerry and I scheduled ours back to back. Deadly serious, Dr. Dixon told me flatly that if being a writer was my dream, I needed to find another dream because I would never be published. "You simply don't have what it takes," he told me, with a sympathy that was contradicted by the sparkling malice in his eyes, "and it would be *criminal* of me to encourage you any further."

He told Jerry the exact same thing.

That night, smoking joints and drinking wine in Jerry's roach-infested apartment, we vowed we would send him copies of our first books when they came out.

When I got my very first box of books, I pulled one out and signed it: *For Dr. Dixon, who told me I'd never be published—still waiting for your first book, asshole. And I hate Henry James. Best wishes, Tracy Norris.*

Oddly enough, I never heard back from him. Go figure.

It took Jerry a little longer to get published, but he wrote a wonderful book about a true crime in the Garden District that hit at just the right time, becoming a runaway best seller and making him enough money to buy a big house and never have to worry about money again. Fifteen years later, the book was still selling a ridiculous number of copies per year in both paperback and hardcover—the ones he'd written since didn't do quite as well, but as he often said, "It's almost impossible to catch lightning in a bottle twice."

"I wonder what ever happened to him? He's not at UNO anymore—I checked. Must have retired," Jerry mused aloud, refilling his glass. His phone chirped again, and he scowled at it. He picked it up and typed on the screen. When he finished, he turned it off and put in his backpack. "You'd think Antinous sold more than a couple hundred copies, the way people are acting. No, I'm not going to cancel the weekend because she died." He sipped his wine. "You said you met her at the airport?"

"In Atlanta." I nodded. "She sat down next to me in the gate area—we were on the same flight. Frankly, I thought she was kind of crazy." The wine was really good, so I refilled my glass. "I mean, straight women are writing gay erotica now? Is that really a thing?" I remembered exactly what she'd said, and sighed. "She said she was bisexual, just too lazy to pursue a woman." I rolled my eyes. "Anyway, I'd never heard of this—what is it—m/m erotica?"

He rolled his eyes. "I don't know that I would call it *erotica*—it's romantic fantasy. No basis in reality." He blew out an exasperated sigh. "Look, I'm all for people writing whatever they want to—I don't want anyone telling me what I can and can't write—but when you're writing about an underprivileged, oppressed class of people, you have a responsibility to them to get it right." He refilled his wineglass. "Imagine if a white woman was writing porn about people of color. Imagine the outrage! But because it's *just* gay men, it's okay."

I reached into my purse and pulled out my copy of *The King's Sword*. "Well, this seemed a bit much to me," I said slowly, staring at the cover design again. The more I looked at it, the more it resembled a parody of an old Rosemary Rogers novel. I put it down on the table.

"Where did you get that?"

"She gave it to me," I replied.

He reached over and picked it up, flipping it open to the title page. "'I hope you enjoy reading this as much as I enjoyed writing it—hope you'll become a fan!'" He choked off a laugh as he opened the book up and started reading aloud. "'Jem's chest heaved, his heart beating so fast and loud he could hear it echoing in his ears, so loud he feared the soldier bathing in the pond might hear it. He peered around the side of the tree trunk he was hiding behind again, and saw that the soldier was standing, his back to him as he scooped water up in both hands and poured it slowly and seductively over his head, the water beading up and running down the milky skin of his back, pooling in the crevasses created by his muscles before streaming into the deep valley between the round scoops of manflesh, that dark indent where the nectar Jem craved was waiting for him.'" He made a retching sound.

I made a face. "That's *horrible*. She did not say 'dark indent where the nectar he craved,' did she? You made that up!"

He shook his head and closed the book. "I wish I was making that up."

I shuddered. "How did that get published?"

"Well—"

"I certainly hope you're going to cancel the rest of this weekend," a voice said.

I looked up, annoyed, to see a man who looked to be in his late forties standing at our table, a scowl on his face. His voice was nasal and high-pitched, grating on me. He was wearing a plaid button-down shirt in various shades of brown that looked incredibly cheap. His stomach strained the lower buttons. The belt on his stained khaki shorts was cinched too tight, so his belly seemed to overflow over the top of it. The shirt wasn't tucked in, either, adding to the overall sloppy appearance. His face was pitted and scarred, and angry red pimples dotted his chin and forehead. His short, curly hair was unkempt, streaked with gray, and looked more than a little greasy. His enormous black plastic-framed glasses were perched halfway down his piglike nose. He hadn't shaved, either.

Jerry smiled, but it didn't quite reach his eyes. I knew that smile—it meant he was holding on to his temper and wanted nothing more than to punch this man, whoever he was, in the face. "Now, Kyle, you know I can't do that."

"It's disrespectful." Kyle spat the words at him, curling his thin upper lip into a sneer. "A writer of Antinous's stature—"

"A writer of Antinous's stature was lucky I included her in the goddamned program in the first fucking place." Jerry's voice was low and his eyes glinted dangerously. "She was a homophobic bitch with little to no talent and a liar on top of everything else." His voice purred as he went on, sending a chill down my spine. "I only included her out of curiosity, you know—to see if she would have the gall to show up after everything she's done."

The man's face reddened. "You'll be sorry—" he started to say, but Jerry cut him off.

"You need to get the fuck away from us." Jerry pushed his chair back and started to stand. "You don't tell me how to run my event, and you're lucky I don't give you the ass-kicking you deserve. Now get out of here before I change my mind."

The interloper opened his mouth but apparently thought better of saying anything and turned on his heel.

I waited a moment before asking, "Who in the hell was that?"

"A troll." Jerry rolled his eyes. "I swear to God, why on earth did I ever think bringing Angels and Demons to New Orleans was a good idea? I swear, gays are our own worst enemies." He sighed and sipped his wine again. "His name is Kyle Bennett—but I call him Vyle. He's horrible." He picked up the book. "You wanted to know who would publish this crap? That's who. He runs a small press called Asgard. He's disgusting—he'll do anything for money. And publishing that bitch was the least of his crimes."

I frowned. "Okay, from what you read I can see that she didn't deserve to be published, but I would hardly call it a crime."

"You know she pretended to be a man for years?" He flipped the book over and put his index finger on the author photo. "That's this model named Dirk Mantooth—mostly does underwear work for gay companies. She hired him to pose for author photos, even to do book signings as her." He sighed. "She started a review website, and with this guy's picture everywhere on it as 'her,' just shredded the work of other writers—mostly books by actual gay male authors—in a horribly nasty and contemptuous way." He clicked his tongue. "For someone who's all about the gay men, she doesn't like real ones very much. And another one of those straight women who'd had enough of being attacked by her on her website outed her over a year ago." He laughed. "As you can imagine, it was quite a little scandal, with people weighing in on both sides—outraged that she'd been outed, as authors 'have a right to privacy,' others saying she was a vicious liar who deserved to be exposed." He put the book back down. "She went after me once." He smiled, his right eyebrow arching upward. "*Once.* Needless to say, she never made *that* mistake again."

"That was incredibly stupid of her." Jerry never forgives and he *never* forgets. Of course, the flip side of that is he will crawl naked on his stomach over broken glass and burning coals for people he cares about.

"Needless to say, I publicly shamed her to the point she publicly apologized to me on her website. Then her publisher dropped her—and Vyle picked her up." His eyes narrowed. "He did that because he knew it would piss me off, of course. So when he suggested I include her in the program, how could I say no?" His eyes glinted again, sending a shiver down my spine. "I felt pretty confident she was going to have a miserable time—I invited some of her biggest online enemies, too." He sighed. "And she was going to be on a panel I'm moderating. I was going to make her sorry she was ever born—but she had to go and kill herself or be murdered or whatever it was that happened to her."

"It had to be murder," I replied, taking another sip of my wine. It really was quite good. I waited for the waitress to put down our plates before continuing, after thanking her, "I'm serious. It wasn't a big enough fall for it to have been suicide or an accident."

"Yeah." He nodded as he started in on his seafood bouillabaisse. "I know. I was just hoping. Murder means the cops are going to be around the rest of the weekend—and that's going to be a royal pain in my ass." He sighed. "If I ever volunteer to organize something like this again, please promise me you'll shoot me once in each temple."

"No good deed." I laughed and started in on my pork chop.

It was delicious.

CHAPTER THREE

I woke up more than a little groggy around seven the next morning.

I was staying in a mini-suite on the eighth floor of the Hotel Monteleone, my favorite hotel in New Orleans. Jerry had graciously gotten me an upgrade, which I greatly appreciated. (It always helps, I find, to be friends with the conference organizer.) The conference was taking place in the meeting areas down on the mezzanine level, and this was the morning everything was starting. My own workshop/master class wasn't until one in the afternoon, and I knew from experience that my nerves would start to get out of control the closer the time came. Teaching an actual class with college students never bothered me, but getting up in front of a room full of people who wanted to be writers for some reason *always* filled me with terror. I always tried to be gracious and encouraging—I had the example of the horror that was Dr. Dixon as a benchmark of what not to be—but I was always afraid I'd give the wrong advice or that someone would point out that I didn't know what the hell I was talking about.

Twelve best-selling mystery novels, several major award nominations, and five popular lesbian romances—and I *still* felt like a fraud calling myself an *author*.

I supposed I would always feel that way.

The mini-suite was absolutely gorgeous—and Jerry had arranged to have a box of chocolate-covered strawberries and a bottle of wine waiting for me in the room when I got back from dinner. I'd had a glass of the wine before bed, sitting on the comfortable sofa in the living room while going over what I'd already written on the new Laura Lassiter novel, hoping against hope that I'd figure out how to end the fucking thing. It hadn't worked—actually the wine I'd had at dinner and the glass in the room had combined to convince me that everything I had already written on the book was garbage.

Not exactly the best mindset to be in before teaching a writing workshop, was it?

I grabbed one of the courtesy robes with the "M" monogrammed in gold thread on the left chest and wandered out into the living room to get a chocolate-covered strawberry. My laptop was sitting on the little desk next to the phone and the room service menu. I hadn't closed it when I'd gone to bed last night, and the black screen glared at me accusingly. I grabbed a strawberry and fled back into the bathroom where the coffeemaker sat on the white marble counter. It was a Keurig, but they'd only given me two of those little K-Cup things—and there was no way two cups of coffee was going to be enough. I was very particular about my coffee—I liked French vanilla creamer rather than the little plastic cups of pseudo half-and-half they'd left for me, but I could deal for this morning. I'd go for a walk after my shower, I decided. There were any number of coffee shops in the French Quarter, and I could stop at the grocery store at Royal and St. Peter for some creamer to keep in the mini-fridge. Hell, they might even have K-Cups I could buy to keep in the room. I turned on a water spigot and filled the coffeemaker, popping one of the little cups into the top, and got it started while I brushed my teeth and washed my face. I popped the strawberry in my mouth as I added the half-and-half and a packet of sweetener to my cup. I ran a brush through my hair while I waited for the coffee to finish brewing. My stomach growled, and I decided to go forage for breakfast on Royal Street as soon as I'd polished off the coffee on hand.

I took a good look at myself in the mirror and moaned. I looked *horrible*. I never sleep well in an unfamiliar bed no matter how tired I am, so despite my exhaustion I'd taken a sleeping pill after the pedi-cab I'd caught in front of Muriel's had dropped me off.

Well, I'd also been afraid of having nightmares. I didn't have them all that often, but when I did they were *awful*. And seriously, I was almost certain to have one the night after a dead body landed almost in my lap.

The coffee was excellent—hot and strong and exactly what I needed. As the caffeine worked its way through my system, the synapses in my brain started firing and brushing away the cobwebs the sleeping pill had left in my head. I closed my eyes and took another delicious sip as I sat back down at the desk in the living room. I quit the writing program and clicked to open my email program—I often find the best time to deal with emails is when I am waking up over my morning coffee. A quick glance through the return addresses of the new ones and I was able to relax—nothing from either editor or agent wondering where the unfinished manuscript was.

I knew I needed to send yet another "I need at least another week" preemptive strike email to the two of them—it's always better to ask for more time before they ask where the manuscript is—but just couldn't face it at the moment. Missing deadlines drove me insane, nagged at me and made me crabby and unpleasant to deal with. For me, missing a deadline was a failure—and there was nothing I loathed more than failing at something.

Anything, really. The therapist I'd seen after I'd fled to the north shore ten years earlier insisted that I needed to come to terms with my fear of failure, and that if I did, when I failed at something it wouldn't cause me "meltdowns" in the future.

I'd smiled at her. "No need to schedule another appointment. I guess I'm a failure at therapy, and I'm fine with it! Amazing progress for only one session! You're a miracle worker."

I walked out and never went back.

I finished going through my emails, and fortunately, there wasn't anything that couldn't wait until later—maybe even until after I'd gotten back to Wilbourne. There were some invitations to speak at writers' conferences, a request for a radio interview, and an offer to speak in the fall to a women's studies program in Alabama—nothing that required an immediate response. I closed the program and opened up a web browser, which automatically defaulted to Facebook. I scrolled through my news feed while finishing the coffee, and yawned.

I am friends with some seriously boring people, I thought as I walked back into the bathroom.

One of the many reasons I don't like to stay in hotels is because usually the bathrooms are tiny and basically useless.

This one at the Hotel Monteleone, on the other hand, was amazing, with an enormous sunken tub with Jacuzzi jets and a glassed-in shower with enough room for at least four or five people, were I so inclined. There was a long marble counter with two sinks, mirrors everywhere, and enough towels for a family. I love taking long, hot showers—really, nothing can quite wake you up in the morning like a long hot shower—and so I turned the water on while my second cup of coffee brewed. I made a mental list of what I wanted to do—make a run to the grocery store to get supplies for the room, a coffee shop and breakfast, check in on the conference, and take a quick browse around the book room.

Half an hour later, with my long blond hair pulled back into a ponytail and wearing white denim shorts and a University of Louisiana-Rouen T-shirt, I walked out the front doors of the hotel and into the swampy heat and humidity. In spite of myself, I couldn't help but smile as I started walking deeper into the Quarter. The cars driving by, the clopping of horse hooves, the milling pedestrians, and the noise—I hadn't quite realized how much I'd missed New Orleans.

Despite the early hour, it was quite warm already, so I was glad I'd decided to make an early-morning run on the errands. I could have lunch in the hotel restaurant, and all the events of the day were inside the hotel—so I wouldn't have to go outside again until dinner. I knew there was a CC's Coffee Shop on Decatur Street, so I turned at the corner and headed toward the river. There was a nice, cool breeze blowing off the Mississippi, carrying the sounds of a calliope on one of the riverboat cruise ships to me.

I'd been born and raised in New Orleans and never thought I'd live anywhere else—and hadn't until I'd gone to grad school at the University of Virginia. I'd been shocked to discover that Mardi Gras wasn't a holiday outside of Louisiana, that bars and liquor stores actually closed, and that other cities' parades kind of sucked. I'd longed to go back, managing to finish my master's and PhD in record time—and getting a tenure-track position at Tulane made it seem like coming home was destiny.

And while I may have fled from New Orleans ten years ago, I *was* still in Louisiana.

But I hadn't realized until that very morning, walking down Bienville Street toward the river, how much I'd missed New Orleans. Rouen was a charming little college town—I liked that it was so quiet, I liked the little subdivision I lived in, and my house was gorgeous, a safe haven where I could relax, write my books, and recharge my batteries. But New Orleans was home, really, and no matter how long I lived in Rouen I'd never feel as connected to it the way I did with this crazy, sleepy, and maddening yet lovable city nestled in a crook of the Mississippi River.

Not for the first time, I wondered if I'd been too hasty in giving up my tenured position at Tulane and moving across the lake.

But on a morning like this, it was easy to believe it had all been a mistake. It wasn't yet hot, my sinuses weren't screaming yet from the thick humidity, and there's nothing as charming as the Quarter in the morning—as long as you stayed away from Bourbon Street. *You didn't make the decision lightly, either,* I reminded myself as I stopped at the corner at Chartres and waited for the line of cars to pass. *You made the best possible decision you could at the time. And you're sane now, aren't you? You would have gone right out of your mind if you'd not left.*

But was that a cop-out?

I couldn't help but wonder about that as I crossed the street and made my way down to Decatur Street. I could smell the river—I'd always loved the river and found some peace by just sitting on the levee and watching the wide expanse of brown water swirling and rushing by the way it had for thousands and thousands of years. It always made me calm and serene, made my problems seem tiny and insignificant.

I decided to take a walk along the levee every morning I was in town.

I was very pleasantly surprised to discover that there wasn't a line at the CC's—apparently I'd missed the on-my-way-to-work morning rush. The place was practically empty, other than a couple of loners reading the newspaper at some tables, and a group farther in the back. I ordered a large cup of house dark roast and an "everything" bagel. I put the bagel through the toaster at the condiment station, and once it was hot and toasted, slathered cream cheese and chives liberally on both halves. I found a small table in the back, near where the small group was having their breakfast, and sighed happily as I sat down. I pulled out my notes as I started eating the bagel. My workshop on The Romantic Hero/Heroine wasn't until one, and even though I knew my material inside and out (I had condensed a week's worth of lectures from my writing class into an hour and fifteen minutes), I preferred to always go over my notes beforehand. I didn't ever want to be one of those tedious instructors who clearly have the lecture memorized and speak in a monotone, boring everyone to tears. I have found that refreshing my memory a few hours ahead of time always seemed to result in a friendly lecture that was not only lively but also encouraged audience participation.

I'd just finished eating my bagel and was quite happily

immersed in my notes when someone at the next table said *Antinous.* My concentration destroyed, I couldn't help but look over at their table.

The group consisted of two men and two women eating some kind of egg and cheese and bagel sandwiches. Each also had an enormous cup of steaming coffee in front of them. It was one of the women who'd said the name, and I noticed they all had lanyards around their necks with name badges dangling at the bottom—clearly they were in town for Angels and Demons.

I decided it wouldn't hurt anyone if I eavesdropped a bit.

"Well," the woman who was speaking continued, "she was such a horrible fucking bitch to so many people, it wouldn't surprise me if it *was* murder after all. It couldn't have happened to a better person. I don't care if she is dead, I hated her and don't mind saying so. When she posted that horrible review of my book, I would have gladly killed her if I had the chance." She had close-cropped red hair gathered into a short ponytail at the base of her neck. I didn't recognize her. Her round face was flushed—whether from the heat or from her own emotional state, I couldn't tell. She was sitting so that she was facing me, and she was smearing butter angrily on the top half of her bagel before replacing it so firmly on top of the sandwich some of the scrambled eggs squirted out on each side. She was a little heavyset, and she wasn't wearing any makeup. A barbed-wire tattoo circled her wrist and a rhinestone stud sparkled in her nose. She was wearing one of those ridiculous *Midnight* T-shirts reading *Team Rolf,* and gold wire-rimmed glasses rested at the end of her nose. "Talk about reaping what you sow. She was always horrible, frankly, even back when she just wrote Twelver fanfic." She sniffed disdainfully. "She was never any good, and she didn't get better when she started writing original fiction." She made air quotes as she said the last two words.

"That's right, I always forget you knew her from back then," the other woman said.

The original speaker started shoving the eggs back into her sandwich. "I wish I'd never known she existed. She was just as horrible on the fan boards as she was on her website. And the fanfic she used to write was disturbing. Not to mention her plagiarism." She compressed her lips together. "Disgusting stuff, really."

"Oh, come on, Pat, the plagiarism charge was never proved," one of the men interrupted. He was balding and heavyset and also wore glasses. The armpits of his black T-shirt were wet, and his reddened forehead was covered with sweat. His voice was deep and booming. "And all of that shit is disturbing. Teachers with underage students—way to play into the stereotype that all gay men are really just pedophiles waiting to get our perverted hands on children." He took another drink of his coffee. "And all that preaching about the cause and everything she'd done for gay equality—when she attacked any and every gay man who dared to write a gay romance. Fucking bitch. I hope she's roasting on a spit in hell."

"Don't be an asshole, Travis." The other woman, a large-breasted brunette with her hair in pigtails on either side of her face, interrupted him. "Just because you don't approve of fanfic doesn't mean it's all bad, or wrong. Some really good writers have come out of fanfic."

"Besides, we're not talking about fanfic, we're talking about Antinous," the redheaded woman, Pat, continued. "I'm not ashamed of my fanfic background. A lot of lesbian romance writers came out of Xena fanfic, for example, and look at *them* now."

"If you mean Aphrodite Longwell, you can just stop right now," Travis responded. "Her stuff is practically a war crime. I've heard she can't go to Europe because she's afraid she'll get dragged before the International Court in the Hague—but no matter what they could do to her, it wouldn't be punishment enough."

That did it. I couldn't help myself. I laughed, and they all turned to look at me.

My laugh is loud and raucous—Jerry swears it can rattle windows—and I gave them an apologetic look. "I'm sorry, I couldn't help overhearing, and that was rather funny. But you're wrong, you know—Aphrodite didn't start with Xena fanfic—she started publishing in the eighties, long before Xena came along." I didn't add that I also thought her fiction was a war crime.

I try to keep my opinions of my colleagues to myself. I don't always succeed, but I do make the effort. I may not respect the final product, but I can respect the amount of work it takes to produce it.

"Oh my God, you're Tracy Norris, aren't you?" Pat's eyes bugged out, and her eyes practically popped out of her round face. She elbowed Travis in the side hard enough for him to grunt. She added smugly, "I *told* you Winter Lovelace and Tracy Norris were the same person, but you never believe anything I say."

"Yes, you're absolutely right." I gave them a slight nod. "Guilty as charged. I am both Tracy Norris and Winter Lovelace."

"You saw her fall, didn't you?" The brunette woman's eyes narrowed as she turned around farther in her chair. "Please tell me she suffered."

"Demi!" Pat shushed her, but the woman was having none of it.

"I'm not going to be a hypocrite and act like I'm sorry she's dead," she insisted. "She was a horrible person and the world is better off without her, you said so yourself." She shrugged. "My name is Demi Filipiak, and this is Pat Greenleaf." She gestured with her head at Travis. "Travis Atkins, and this other fool's name is Mike Burton."

"Nice to meet you all," I replied, smiling. "And no, Demi, I didn't actually *see* her fall. I just saw her land." I shuddered, hearing it again in my head. "It was kind of unpleasant, actually."

"We're actually all going to be in your workshop this afternoon." Pat's smile didn't waver a bit—and I recognized the look in her eyes. She was starstruck, which always makes me uncomfortable because I hardly consider myself to be a star. I'm not Sue Grafton or Sara Paretsky, for God's sake. "And I'm really looking forward to it. I mean, I'm a big fan of your work as Winter Lovelace, but I really love, love, love the Laura Lassitter series. I wish I'd been sure you were the same person because I'd have brought my copies to have them signed." She blinked at me a few times, and her smile was getting so big it had to hurt. "It's amazing how different the lesbian romances are from the mysteries! You'd never know the same person wrote both. You really are a master at writing."

"Thank you—I tried to make sure they're very different." I was pleased. It's always lovely to meet someone who reads your work when you're in a non-embarrassing environment.

There's nothing worse than having someone approach you when you're somewhere like a public restroom, or when you're buying tampons at the drugstore and the cashier recognizes you. "I hope you enjoy the workshop. Are you all romance writers?"

"I'm not," Mike Burton said while the others nodded. He had mousy brown hair and was really slender—his arms were covered with colorful tattoos. He was wearing a Metallica T-shirt, which kind of took me aback. *Get over yourself—gay men can like heavy metal, they don't all like Lady Gaga and Madonna.* "I write mysteries, but I figured there's a lot of similarities between romances and mysteries, and character is character." He shrugged. "Writing's writing, right?"

Before I could answer him, Pat quickly asked, "When is the next Laura Lassiter coming out?"

I have to finish writing it first. "Not until next February, I'm afraid."

"That long?" Pat's face fell. She blew out her breath in disappointment.

I steered the conversation back around to Antinous. "I was rather curious about Antinous," I said slowly. "You say she came out of fanfic?"

Demi nodded. "Yes, that's where Pat and I met her. She wrote primarily the creepy stuff—you know, like the werewolf brothers having three-ways with the master mage, that kind of stuff. That's the problem with fandom, if you ask me. People will write this really revolting stuff but you can't really kick them out of the groups, you know? I mean, we're all really just fans, and who's to say whose fiction is okay and whose isn't? I started reading it all because, you know, I devoured the books and just couldn't wait for the next one to come out—"

"Like your Laura books," Pat interrupted.

"There's not Laura fanfic, is there?" I asked, frowning a little bit. It had never occurred to me that some of my readers might want to create their own Laura adventures, and now that it *had* occurred to me, I wasn't sure how I felt about it, to be honest.

My gut feeling was that I didn't like it one bit.

Laura was *my* character, damn it!

"There might be." Demi shrugged. "I've never looked for it."

Ouch.

"Antinous was one of those people who try to take over everything, you know, like they appoint themselves as arbiters of what's good and what's not, and God fucking forbid you disagree with anything she says." Travis made a face. "I wrote some fanfic, yes, but mine wasn't *erotic*."

"Erotic?" *The werewolf brothers having three-ways with the master mage.* I felt a little nauseous. "So what you're saying is there's *Midnight* porn? She wrote *Midnight* Twelver porn?"

"Not all of it is erotic," Travis insisted, turning a little red. "I just wrote, you know, adventures in addition to what was already in the canon—adventures some of the lesser characters had while the main ones were having their big adventures that, you know, the minor characters weren't involved in. It was good practice for writing my own fiction. I wrote a couple of those, and then people liked them and I thought maybe I should try my hand at original stuff." He smiled proudly. "I sold my very first non-fanfic short story, and I've been writing ever since."

"That's terrific!" I beamed at him, thinking it might be an interesting exercise for one of my writing classes when I was back at ULR in the fall. *It could actually be an excellent exercise for character building—dissect an actual character from published fiction, write a little scene for them.*

"Antinous, of course, trashed my first novel." He scowled. He reached into his backpack and pulled out a book, which he passed over to me.

I looked at it and fought not to smile. It was the typical gay male book cover—a muscular headless man with no shirt or body hair, the top button of his jeans undone so the waistband of his underwear was exposed. Behind him was a bed with the figure of another man facedown on it, the sheet down so far I could see the crack of his ass. In flowing script were the words *To Love Again* and across the bottom was the name *Travis Atkins*. Under the name were the words *Best-selling author of "Love Is a Rose."* I turned it over and read the brief description on the back:

> *After Roman's first love was killed in a tragic accident, he never dreamed he would ever find love again. Shutting himself off from his friends and family, Roman throws himself into his work to forget his grief. Until the handyman he hires to do some repair work on his house shows up one day, and Roman starts having those feelings again...*
>
> *Will Roman take a chance on having his heart broken again?*

It sounded like the set-up of a gay porn movie—and not one of the good ones.

Oh, because the plot of your latest romance novel is groundbreaking? Stop being such a bitch.

I passed it back to Travis with a smile. "It sounds wonderful. Congratulations."

He practically simpered. "Oh," he pushed it back into my hands, "you can keep it. I'd consider it an honor." Then he grabbed it back and pulled a Sharpie out of his pocket. "I'll sign it for you." He opened it up, scribbled something on the title page, and shoved it back at me with a huge smile on his face.

I didn't want it, but I also didn't want to be rude, so I slipped it into my bag. "Thank you."

"Please let me know what you think of it," he went on. "My website's in my bio on the back cover, and you can email me there."

"Like she doesn't have anything better to do than read your book and give you a critique," Pat responded with a rather snarky laugh.

Travis looked stricken, and I could have slapped her. Instead, I just gave her a little frown and said, "You said Antinous was problematic in fandom, didn't you?"

"Oh, she was *horrible*." Demi shook her head. "Absolutely horrible. Mean and nasty like you wouldn't believe, always complaining about how this story or that story wasn't 'authentic.' That was her big thing, you know—saying books and stories weren't 'authentic.'" She smirked. "And all that time she was pretending to be a man. And even after she started writing original fiction, she was *always* dinging other writers for not writing 'authentic' stories about gay men. Like somehow she was the authority on being authentic." She rolled her eyes theatrically. "Because of course the biggest authority on gay authenticity is a woman pretending she's a man."

"And she was misogynist enough to be convincing—I really thought she was a man." Pat picked up the story from there. "I mean, some of the stuff she would say about other authors—and readers—was just unbelievably horrible. And then she decided to write her own books, and then she'd come on the boards and mock us for writing our fanfic while *he, she, whatever,* you know, was really doing amazing original work and getting these huge advances for her historical romances. Bragging and taunting us. And if anyone struck back at her, she'd get all hurt and offended and weepy about how mean people were being to her." She snapped her fingers. "She could dish it out in spades but she couldn't take it."

"She actually talked about how much money she made?" I couldn't wrap my mind around it. No authors I knew would *ever* talk about money except in the most broad and general ways. I was also raised to believe that talking about money was something you just didn't do, ever.

"Bitch, please—everything she said was a lie." Mike leaned forward in his chair. "The publisher she was working with didn't pay advances—well, neither publisher she worked with. Kyle Bennett and Asgard certainly don't. They don't do any editing, either, or copy-editing. Pretty much the way you turned in the book was how it went to print. I mean, the press I'm with might not pay advances, but at least I have an editor and the books get copy-edited."

"And her first publisher went out of business—went bankrupt." Demi laughed nastily. "I mean, she was always bragging on her blog and everywhere about her enormous sales and how much money she was making and all the fan email she got, but if that was the case, why did her publisher go bankrupt? And if he was bankrupt, how was she getting paid her enormous royalties? And of course when she signed up with Asgard, she started posting nasty stuff about her old publisher."

"The best, though, was when she was outed as a straight woman." Travis grinned. "It was so awesome. After using her website and her blog to trash people for years, like I said, and rip other people's books to shreds as not being authentic—she said terrible stuff about how straight women couldn't write authentic gay romance novels, and then she accused another author—who'd given an interview about how her teenaged son's coming-out struggle had inspired her to write young adult fiction about gay teens—well, Antinous blasted her for 'using her son's experience for her own profit' and things like that. The nastiest, most hateful stuff imaginable."

"Leslie MacKenzie," Pat interjected. "And a lovelier woman you've never met. She's a really good writer, too. She's here this weekend."

Interesting.

"So, one of Leslie's fans was connected to Antinous's first publisher somehow, I don't really know how it all came about," Mike picked up the story, "and the fan *exposed* her publicly—got a scan of her signature page on the book contract, which of course was in her real name—and then tracked down the model she'd been using for her author photos and author appearances, and got *him* to admit he wasn't a writer."

"I imagine that must have been quite a scandal," I replied slowly.

"Oh, it was like someone had thrown a grenade into the Internet." Pat shook her head sadly. "Everyone she'd been horrible to went after her with torches and pitchforks, and then other people tried to defend her, and it was just this big blow-up. And then she claimed that she used a male name because she was actually trans…"

"Which really pissed me the fuck off because I *am* trans," Pat snapped. "And how *dare* she appropriate the identity of transpeople? To give herself credibility? The fucking bitch."

"She told me she was bisexual," I replied.

All four of them looked at me.

"We were on the same flight from Atlanta," I explained. "She sat next to me in the gate area, and she kind of told me the story—not like this, of course. She told me she was actually bisexual, but just too lazy to ever try to be with another woman."

They exchanged glances. "I *told* you she wasn't trans," Demi said smugly, folding her arms and leaning back in her chair. "It was just her scurrying for cover, trying to excuse her lies."

"I don't know why she felt the need to lie in the first place," Mike said. "It's not like the romance community isn't full of straight women writing gay romances. It wasn't a big deal that she was a straight woman—the problem was that she actively lied and perpetrated a fraud, and under the guise of that fraud, she attacked other writers." He shook his head. "She claimed her publisher made her do it. But her publisher didn't make her go after other writers. Her publisher didn't make her act like a complete bitch online."

"Did this come out before or after she started publishing with Kyle Bennett?" I asked.

"I think she went to Asgard after?" Demi shook her head. "I can't remember."

I shook my head. "Funny how when J. T. LeRoy claimed to be a gay man, and hired actors to play the role in public to perpetuate the fraud, she got drummed out of publishing."

"Exactly!" Mike put his fist up so I could give him a bump with mine. "J. T. LeRoy was driven out of the business completely for lying about being a gay man. But not Antinous. That bitch was defiant and nasty to the very end." He made a face. "Yeah, the world's a better place without her."

"Christ, look at the time," Travis interrupted. "We're going to be late if we don't go."

They all got up quickly, and there was a flurry of "see you at your workshop" and "it was so lovely to meet you" and so forth before they made their way out of the coffee shop.

I sat there for a few minutes more, thinking.

Chapter Four

About an hour before my workshop was to start, I closed my laptop with a sigh and leaned back in the desk chair.

I was really behind on my book, but somehow I just couldn't make myself work on it. I just sat there staring at the screen and the goddamned blinking cursor. Three chapters more was all I needed, and I could turn the damned thing in and get paid. I'd never had this much trouble with a novel before—and the deadline for my next lesbian romance was looming; it was due in less than six months. It was driving me insane. I knew it was there in my subconscious, but I couldn't figure out how to get it out and onto the page. I just stared at the screen, wishing I was one of those authors who had the discipline to do an outline and then stick to it. I used to outline in the very beginning, until around my third book, when I realized that there was such a huge difference between the outline and the final manuscript that a stranger wouldn't recognize the finished book from reading the outline. After that, I'd stopped outlining my novels because it was clearly a waste of my time. And I'd never had any problem finishing a book, until now. For some reason, I had no idea how to get Laura out of the jam she was in, figure out who the killer was, and somehow kill off her latest love interest.

Of course, Laura couldn't figure out who the killer was because I didn't know. This was not a good thing. From the very beginning, I hadn't the slightest idea who'd murdered New Orleans socialite Rebecca Stroud. I'd just plowed ahead, figuring I'd figure it out when I got there the way I always did. Only now I was there and I didn't have a fucking clue who'd killed her. I'd reread the manuscript I don't know how many times, to no avail. I'd pored over my character list and their bios, but every time I thought, *Yes, he's the killer,* when I started to write it all out it didn't make sense and seemed trite, boring, unoriginal—something I'd done before.

Two months past deadline—something that had never happened to me before in my entire career. Not once had I turned in a manuscript late. I always turned everything in promptly, did my edits and revisions in a timely manner, and got the page proofs turned back in well ahead of time.

What the hell is wrong with me?

I needed to get this book finished so I could start the next one or else I was going to be in the same situation again.

Maybe you shouldn't write two books a year anymore.

It was a conundrum I'd found myself in before. I loved writing, but it was draining, both emotionally and physically exhausting. I started writing the romances as a break from the hard-boiled, somewhat depressing world of Laura Lassiter. Her world was bleak, she dealt with the dregs of humanity, and she'd become more and more cynical with every book. Who could blame her, though, the way her love interests always wound up dead by the last page? This current one was almost too hard for me to write because the subject matter was so dark that I'd found myself drinking too much to get my mind out of that horrible place. There were nights when I'd drown myself in wine, sit in the comfortable living room of my little place at Wilbourne College and could finally understand why Hemingway had shot himself.

The romances weren't angst-ridden, of course. I saw myself as writing lesbian chick-lit, romantic comedies with sparkling dialogue and wit and humor that ended happily ever after with my two heroines riding off into the sunset together. I modeled them after those wonderful Cary Grant and Katharine Hepburn movies from the 30s and 40s, like *Bringing Up Baby* and *The Philadelphia Story*. And readers responded to them. I didn't get thousands of emails at my Winter Lovelace Gmail account or on her Facebook page the way Antinous had claimed to, but I got quite a few.

Those books were about as different from the mysteries as humanly possible. The romances were the way I wanted the world to be; the mysteries were the world as I knew it to be.

Little wonder I couldn't make myself go into the mindset I needed to work on *The Jade Tiger: A Laura Lassiter Mystery.*

Instead, I'd just spent the entire morning researching Antinous Renault online.

And what a treasure trove of horror that had turned out to be!

I rubbed my eyes and stood up, arching my back until it cracked and the lower back muscles, which had tightened while I sat there, loosened up a bit.

I got a can of Diet Coke out of the mini-fridge and walked over to the window of my suite's little living room. I pulled back the curtains and looked out over the French Quarter. The sun was out in force now, and I could practically see the steam rising from the streets.

When I'd gotten back to my room after running my errands, I'd sat down intending to work on the book. But I couldn't shake the image of Antinous and her glassy eyes staring at me as the blood pooled around her cracked head. I figured it wouldn't hurt to nose around online, see what I could find out about her for a little while before diving headfirst back into the book. I was relatively certain she couldn't possibly be as bad as Jerry and the others had said she was in the coffee shop.

No one could be that awful, right? They had to be exaggerating.

Boy, was I wrong.

The sad truth was they hadn't even scratched the surface of the horror that had called itself Antinous Renault—and once I started, I got sucked into the Internet vortex completely and there was no coming back out.

Excuses, excuses. You just don't want to work on the book.

And you know the real reason why you started writing two books a year, you can just stop lying to yourself. You started writing two books a year because you needed to keep busy so you wouldn't think about—

Determinedly I stopped that train of thought in its tracks, as I did every time my mind tried to go there.

Antinous's murder was a fine distraction from those treacherous thoughts.

The first link in the web search I did took me to her blog, which she'd called *Erased from History*. I smiled to myself— I'd used that very phrase with her myself at the airport. *What could it hurt,* I asked myself, *to read a few entries?* The most recent one had been posted just a few days earlier, and in it she talked about how excited she was to be coming to America for the first time, and how thrilled she was to be on two panels at Angels and Demons—which she referred to as "the TOP GLBT writers' conference in the world." I did roll my eyes a little—hasn't the battle over the order of the letters been over for a while, with the agreement that the L goes first? *Typical straight woman,* I thought with a shake of my head.

I read about her having to board her cats (all named after *Midnight* characters, of course), and what should she pack, and what should she see and where should she eat in New Orleans. It was poignant, and I felt sympathy for the poor deluded thing. I could remember the first time I'd ever gone to something similar as a published author—Bouchercon, right after my first Laura mystery had come out—and how nervous and excited I was. No one, of course, had the slightest idea of who I was there, and it was a bit unnerving to sit at the mass signing and sign two copies of my book while other authors had enormous lines that snaked out the door. The fact that she was so excited about the trip just three days ago, a trip where she was getting to be, in her own words, "an author in public for the first time" was just so sad, given that she'd been killed and never gotten to experience it. She might have been the most horrible person who'd ever lived, but every author should get to experience that at least once in their life.

That feeling faded rather quickly when I got to her next entry.

But awful as her blog entries were, I couldn't stop reading them. It was like eating potato chips or smoking crack. And for a crime writer, they were *fascinating.*

Her blog was one of the most fascinating examples of narcissism and self-delusion I'd ever seen—so much so that I bookmarked it so I could go back and reference it whenever I needed to. There were instances when I was so amazed at her utter lack of self-awareness that I had to reread what she'd written several times. It was a fascinating view into a particular mindset that I might be able to use for a future Laura novel. There were times when I found myself thinking, *It's not shocking that someone killed her—the shocking part is it TOOK THIS LONG.* I kept reading, going further and further back in time, unable to tear myself away from her psychosis.

I used to blog on my website, but my entries had gotten fewer and further between as the years went by—it was incredibly hard to find safe topics to write about. I didn't want to use my blog solely for self-promotion, something I was never completely comfortable with—there was an element of sideshow freak hawking snake oil to it that made me squeamish. Antinous's blog was the perfect example of what I didn't want to do. I couldn't see how this encouraged people to go out and buy her books, or even *like* her. She came across as a smug know-it-all, and whiny—the posts she made in response to bad reviews were basically public pity parties: *feel sorry for me, if you love my books please go defend me and attack the reviewer, poor, poor pitiful me.* It made me wince for her. It was pretty clear that outside of her cats, she really didn't have any real-life friends. There was no one to go have lunch with or have over for tea. The Internet was the extent of her contact with the outside world, which made me rather sad for her. Occasionally she would mention her late parents, but no siblings, no neighbors, no real-life people she interacted with other than her doctor—whom she raged against because he always told her she needed to lose weight.

It made me really happy I'd never blogged regularly.

Of course, now the "experts" on publishing said blogging was over and the best way to promote your books was on social media. I had an author page on Facebook where I made announcements about signings and appearances and good reviews and so forth—all the things the publicist at my publisher said I needed to post—but I tried not to engage with people on there. I heard so many horror stories from other authors…and reading this woman's blog just confirmed that my decision to limit my exposure to social media was the right one for me. I decided it was probably a good idea not to check out Antinous's Facebook page or her Twitter account.

Her vitriolic entries about other writers were the worst.

And her "friends" always rose to the occasion, giving her the praise she so desperately craved whenever she posted about some reviewer or other author being nasty to her. It was also, I noted, always the same group of about four or five people—which kind of gave the lie to her claim that she had thousands of fans.

It also blew my mind how she frequently played "victim" in some entries when in others she was absolutely vile and hateful about another writer—the kind of thing we always think about writers we don't like, but *never* say publicly.

Clearly, she'd never taken the course on how not to burn bridges in publishing.

She was also pretty scathing about some publishers she'd worked with—again giving the lie to her claims of enormous success; if she sold as many books as she'd claimed, would these small presses I'd never heard of have folded?

And then there were her entries about the "gay male experience"—the "Cause," as she called it, which reminded me of how the Southerners in *Gone with the Wind* referred to the Confederacy—which was fine. I didn't have a problem with straight women as allies—we'd never get anywhere as queers without our straight allies. But she never talked about anyone other than gay men—never the transgendered (which she had, according to one entry, claimed to be at one time) or bisexuals (which she also claimed to be) or lesbians. Gay men, in their privilege as male, often neglected the other letters in the alphabet soup of the queer community, which was of course wrong but could be expected because of being born with a penis in a sexist world.

But she *wasn't a gay man.*

She was very clear, on multiple occasions, about being too lazy to pursue attractions with women although the attractions were enough for her to claim bisexual status. *I say I am, so therefore I am despite everything to the contrary.*

And no one ever called her on it—no one questioned it.

So, I thought, *I could, despite the fact that I've never had sex with a man and have only been in relationships with women, claim to be straight and people just have to accept it? That's fucking crazy.*

I kept reading, going backward through time, until I finally reach this tearful entry:

15 January

I want to thank everyone for their well-wishes and kind emails and messages over the last week or so. After the initial depression—and all of the attendant nastiness that came with the HORRIBLE, vile personal attack on me and my work last week, you've all bloody well made me feel like I can go on living. I cannot express my gratitude enough about the way you, my wonderful wonderful fans, have rallied around me in this, my time of tribulation. All I have done, it seems, for the past few days is cry.

*Just when I think all of my tears have dried up, that
I couldn't possibly cry any more, the horrible cruelty
of this vicious personal attack on me overwhelms me
again and I collapse back onto my sofa and sob until
my sides ache.*

I rolled my eyes—if her fiction was only half as
melodramatic as her blog, it would be unreadable.

> *Yes, I am a biological woman and not a gay man.
> Yes, it is true that I hired an actor to do signings and
> readings for me in the States as well as to pose for
> my author photos. My original publisher insisted
> that no one would read m/m if it was written by a
> woman, and when he came up with the idea of hiring
> Dirk Mantooth to play Antinous Renault in public, I
> foolishly went along with it.*
>
> *Yes, it was a deception but it was done in the
> PUREST sense with the PUREST of hearts—*

Right, I thought, rolling my eyes so hard they almost
popped out of my head as I read it.

> *—and there was no malicious intent, despite all the
> horrible accusations that have been hurled at me
> since that horrible Anne Howard and her friends
> TARGETED me for abuse last week. Once the
> deception was started, I could not think how to bring
> it to a logical close. I couldn't think of how to respond
> to any of these vicious attacks without adding fuel
> to the fire. I kept hoping that having collected their*

pound of flesh, they would be satisfied to finally end their gloating and find someone else to try to destroy emotionally and professionally, as they have done to me so horribly and relentlessly. This is why I allowed the torture to go on unchecked, without giving any of it the dignity of a measured response, which is more than this witch hunt deserves. But I have come to realize, when I am not so horribly depressed that all I can do is cry, is that my silence gives credence to their vicious accusations. That in not standing up to these horrible bullies, I am allowing them to win, and I will NOT surrender to such people. Not when poor gay teenagers are killing themselves out of despair from the bullying they endure from their homophobic peers. I realized that I MUST speak out, that I MUST stand up for them, that I cannot allow such indecent and horrible conduct to get the best of me, just as gay men cannot allow the vicious attacks of the fundamentalist Christians and their minions in positions of political power to silence them and push them back into the closet after all the years of hard work. I will not be silenced.

As for the spurious charges of deception, of course all anyone had to do was check the copyright office and they would have seen for themselves that Antinous Renault was, indeed, a woman and not a gay man.

But since my outing—

If she weren't already dead, comparing being exposed as a fraud and a liar to the horrific struggle every queer goes through would have made me want to kill her. And to compare what happened to *her* to the suicides of bullied queer youth?

That made me want to piss on her grave. Why *did* it take so long for someone to kill this monster?

> *—I've realized that now I am free from this minor deception and can now go forth as myself, a biological female, and what an enormous relief that is! You have no idea how many times I have wanted to come out publicly as myself and put a stop to all of this nonsense. I have always stood for truth and honesty and authenticity, and despite the pretense, have been my true self here, in my fiction, and on my review website. And of course knowing that so many readers and friends throughout the world love me, understand my struggle and what I am going through and want nothing but the best for me—well, I'm practically in tears all over again, but not in sadness and depression but rather for your incredible kindnesses! And this outing has made me understand the GLBT—*

Again with the letters not in the proper order! I suppose it shouldn't come as a surprise that a straight woman had no idea that lesbians had fought long and hard to not have secondary status—a status that apparently straight English bitches appropriating the gay male experience for profit feel is all we deserve.

> *—process even more, the struggle that every GLBT human goes through their entire life until they can finally be honest with themselves and the world. And*

since I am being honest about everything here, I may
as well be completely honest and confess to you all
that I believe I may actually be transgendered.

That made my blood boil so hot I had to get up and walk around before I could continue reading.

What exactly had she said to me in the airport yesterday? That she was bisexual but had never had sex with a woman because she was too lazy?

Killing *had* been too good for her.

So, the gay male experience wasn't enough for her to appropriate—she had to appropriate the transgender and bisexual ones as well?

Hateful fucking bitch.

It took me a while to calm down before I could read again—but after that, I was pretty much prepared for anything else completely insane she might claim.

After reading back several more months, I moved on from the blog to her website.

There was very little—if any—middle ground with Antinous. She either loved a book or she absolutely loathed it—and there were very few books, apparently, that she loved.

And when she loathed a book, she went after it with everything she had, including the kitchen sink.

This author should be haunted by the ghosts
of the trees killed to print this garbage...this book
should be used as an example of what not to do in
writing courses...I wanted to throw this across the
room but didn't want to risk damaging my Kindle...I

wouldn't use the pages of this book to wipe my ass
because it would be an insult to my ass…

And other charming bon mots like that. Dorothy Parker she wasn't.

My personal favorite was a vicious takedown of a book where she used the review to speak directly to the author—a gay man I'd actually known who'd committed suicide two years before she savaged his book:

> *Really, Mr. Severn? That was the best you could*
> *come up with? Shame, shame, shame on you! You*
> *really should put a little more thought and creativity*
> *into your work before you foist it upon the reading*
> *public, Mr. Severn.*

I just hoped Chris Severn's surviving partner hadn't seen this smug dismissal of his work. Chris had even written a brilliant, award-winning memoir about his years-long struggle with depression.

Again, she was lucky she was already dead before I read this cruel and dismissive attack on a dead man's work.

But the worst was yet to come.

This was an attack on another writer—Leslie MacKenzie—who was writing young adult novels with gay characters and stories. The woman apparently had a gay son who was a teenager.

> *I find it abhorrent that someone would take*
> *ADVANTAGE of her son's sexuality and true life*
> *experiences to make money and build a career for*

herself. What kind of mother would exploit their child like that? Where are the American children's services people to take this child away from a mother who would do something as despicable and horrible as this? This is so vile it beggars description...as you can be certain, dear friends, I will NOT review this horrible woman's work and give it a forum or ANY publicity of any kind, and the only reason I mention her name is so that you, too, can AVOID her books like the plague they are...one had to wonder, does she question her son about his dating habits? Does she spy on him when he's being intimate with another boy? This just frankly reeks of pedophilia at best, child pornography at worst...it also makes me wonder if the child actually does in fact exist...or if she simply invented a gay son to give her "work" more credibility, an authenticity it doesn't deserve, hmmm? Friends, we have all seen that there are SOME writers who will do ANYTHING to get attention for their books rather than letting their books be judged on their own merits.

EDIT* I have shut the comments on this entry down, and deleted the ones that were already posted. While I am certainly the biggest advocate of free speech, I will not allow fans of this despicably vile woman to come here and attack me in the ways that they were doing! I find it incredibly horrible that a group of heterosexual white women would attack a gay man in such a way! So, I will henceforth have no choice but to moderate all comments, and ban people who come

*here with ad hominem attacks on me. Shame on you
all, you homophobic BITCHES.*

Considering she was a straight woman pretending to be a
gay man—I shook my head. Despicable, really. If this was the
kind of thing she regularly engaged in, no wonder she was so
reviled.

It was amazing she'd left it up after she was exposed for
the whole world to see.

Then again, as I'd already noted, self-awareness wasn't
her strong suit.

She was an unspeakably vile piece of garbage, and after
reading it all, I felt like I needed a shower.

*I would have stayed away from this conference if I were
her,* I thought as I closed the curtains. *Why would she come to
something like this?*

*She clearly liked the attention—even the negative.
Negative attention is better than no attention, I guess, for
people like her.*

I put the Diet Coke down on the desk as I walked through
the bedroom back into the enormous bathroom.

But the name Leslie MacKenzie sounded familiar—so
did Anne Howard, for that matter.

I tried to remember where I'd heard the names before as
I turned on the hot water and washed my face. I rinsed my
mouth out with some of the mouthwash provided by the hotel,
which wasn't bad. I took some deep breaths and cleared my
mind, pushing the murder of the incredibly unpleasant woman
and her online rantings out of my head once and for all.

Not bad for forty-five, I thought as I ran a brush through my
long blond hair one last time. I'd spent most of my life trying

to stay out of the sun, so my skin was still fresh-looking and smooth. I only had a few, almost unnoticeable lines radiating out from my eyes and the corners of my mouth. I didn't look like I was in my twenties—I'm not that delusional—but I still looked well put together. I'd been an athlete in high school and had never really gotten out of the habit of staying fit. One of the things I disliked about Wilbourne's brutal winter was having to jog on a treadmill at the campus fitness center rather than outside on the roads. I'd tried being a vegetarian for a while, but bacon defeated me. I still limited my intake of red meat, but every once in a while I gave in to the siren song of a bacon cheeseburger. The pale-blue blouse and gray slacks I'd chosen gave me a nice, professional air. I checked my shoulder bag for my notes, laptop, and iPad, and swept out of the room.

I took the elevator down to the mezzanine level. There was a pair of long tables set up across from the elevator bank; the one on the left had a sign reading *Information* while the one on the right said *Check-In*. Two women sat at each table—I didn't recognize any of them, and Jerry was nowhere to be seen.

I smiled and hitched my shoulder bag back up. "Good afternoon," I said to the women at the Check-In table. "I'm Winter Lovelace, and I think I need to check in?"

The two women, who were hunched over an iPad playing some game involving moving jewels around, both looked up with wide eyes.

"Oh my God," one of them spluttered. She looked to be the older of the two—maybe in her late fifties or so. She was wearing a gray sweatshirt with *Angels and Demons* on the front. She reached down and pulled up a book bag, which she set on the table. "I have your books! I am such a fan! Would

you mind signing them for me? Jo, get her registration packet!"
While the other woman retrieved an envelope and a gift bag
for me, the first woman, whose name tag read *Charlene,*
reverently placed pristine copies of my four romance novels
on the table.

I grabbed a black Sharpie from the side pocket of my
shoulder bag and knelt down to sign the books. I picked up
the first one, *Love Is In The Air,* and examined it. It looked
brand new; the spine was intact. I opened it up to the title page.
"Would you like me to personalize it?" I always ask, since I
made the mistake of signing a book once to someone who then
snapped, "Signature only! You've *ruined* it!" I'd bought that
person another copy, and always asked from then on.

"Yes, that would be so lovely!" she breathed. "Make it to
Charlene, C-H-A-R-L-E-N-E."

"Or she could look at your name tag," Jo said rather
snidely.

"Yes, yes, of course." Charlene's face turned scarlet.
"Listen to me, you must think I'm a blithering idiot. I'm just
such a huge fan…I've read all of your books so many times.
I bought new ones," she went on as I signed the first one and
opened the second, "because I didn't want you to see how badly
I'd abused the original ones I had. Oh, this is such a thrill!"
she gushed. "As soon as I heard you were coming to Angels
and Demons, I knew I had to come meet you." Her chest was
heaving, and although her blush had faded, there were two
spots of color on her cheeks. "Listen to me blather on, you
must think I'm the biggest idiot in the world, seriously."

Before I could answer Jo snapped, "A little late to be
worried about that now, isn't it?"

I looked up from *Love Under the Bleachers* and raised an
eyebrow. "Are you two a couple, by any chance?"

Jo had the decency to blush, and bit her lower lip. She nodded.

I finished signing the books and handed them back to Charlene, who blushed again. I held out my hand and shook hands with both of them, adding it was a pleasure to meet them, and wandered into the little room right off the foyer, which a sign declared to be the *Book Room*. I instantly recognized the man behind the tables piled high with books. He was scowling at a young man with longish brown hair sticking out from underneath a black beret; he was tall and skinny, was wearing beltless jeans defying gravity to stay up and a ratty-looking old green T-shirt. The young man looked vaguely familiar.

"If I have to tell you one more time to stop, I'll have hotel security throw you out," the man behind the table said in a "I've had enough of your nonsense" tone.

"You shouldn't be carrying that bitch's books anyway," the young man snarled before turning and storming out of the room, almost knocking me down in his hurry to get out. I wasn't able to get a look at his face, other than he had glasses taped together over his nose and some pimples on his chin.

"Ted!" Ted worked at the Prytania Bookshop, a wonderful independent store in the little mall at the corner of Washington and Prytania in the Garden District. I've known Ted for years. He's funny, a big sports buff (we often emailed back and forth about the Saints), and very well read. If Ted recommended a book, I bought it without question. He also wrote an anonymous blog about the book business that was one of the funniest things I've ever read.

He smiled at me. "I was wondering when you were going to stick your nose in here."

"What was that about?" I asked, my eyebrows coming together over my nose.

Ted sighed. "He keeps coming in here and piling other people's books on top of these." He gestured with his left hand to two stacks of books—*The King's Sword* and *His Majesty's Pleasure,* both by none other than Antinous Renault. "And when I told him to stop—well, you heard him. I guess he's not a fan."

"Apparently not," I replied, looking back out the door, but the young man had apparently disappeared. "Antinous Renault seemed to have that effect on a lot of people."

"No one seems to want to buy her books," Ted replied glumly. "I thought what with the tragic death and all, there'd be some morbid curiosity—you know how people are, they'd be able to show it to people and say, I bought it that weekend in New Orleans when she was murdered." He looked at me over the top of his glasses. "You found the body, I heard?"

I nodded. "Not so much found as it landed in front of me." I quickly gave him a brief overview of what happened, leaving out having met her at the airport and the things I'd since found out about her.

"Awful." He clicked his tongue. "You want to sign your books while you're here?"

I found my Winter Lovelace romances stacked neatly at a corner where two different tables had been pushed together. Right next to them, the Tracy Norris mysteries were stacked neatly. I tapped my finger on the stack of the most recent, *Blood on the Bayou.* "Have any people figured out that Winter and Tracy are the same person?" I couldn't stop myself from giving him a conspiratorial wink.

Ted laughed. "I've had a couple of people asking why I

was stocking the mysteries, if Tracy was going to be here—and they didn't believe me when I said Tracy and Winter were the same person. I just compared the author photos for them… and that did the trick."

"Did they buy anything?"

"One seemed kind of pissed to find out, honestly." Ted shrugged. "'If I'd known Tracy Norris was really Winter Lovelace I would have brought my copies from home!'"

I sighed. As much as I loved being a writer, sometimes readers could be a bit of a challenge. But if it weren't for them I'd be just a professor of English at a small university in the middle of nowhere in Louisiana, so as frustrating as they could be sometimes, I always had to suck it up.

I was *lucky* to be published in the first place.

And no, it doesn't suck to have people tell you regularly that you're brilliant.

The trick is not to start believing it yourself—therein lies the path to madness.

And almost as if on cue, the personification of that walked into the book room, followed by a coterie of her adoring readers.

My heart sank. The last person in the world I ever wanted to run into was Aphrodite Longwell.

"Winter darling!" she said in her phoniest voice as she threw her arms apart and clacked across the marble floor in her high-heeled pumps.

I suppose in the interest of full disclosure I have to confess that I had an interlude of sorts with Aphrodite years ago—when I was young and foolish and didn't know any better.

I learned the hard way.

And in fairness, I have to admit Aphrodite looked good for her age. I wasn't sure just how old Aphrodite actually was, but I knew for a fact she was older than me. She always kept her hair cut short in what I always thought of as the Shirley Partridge style, and it was always either dyed platinum blond or had streaks of blond through it. Currently she'd gone platinum, and she was, as always, wearing too much makeup— the rouge was thickly applied and her lips were painted the same shade. Her eye shadow was a sparkly green, and she had thickly mascaraed long eyelashes that had to be fake. She was wearing a tight pair of jeans under a pink silk blouse with the belt so tightly cinched it looked like the circulation to her legs might be cut off.

Okay, that was rather harsh—but it *was* pulled pretty damned tight.

Aphrodite referred to herself as the goddess of lesbian romance, and she did have a large and incredibly loyal fan base. No one knew if Aphrodite Longwell was her real name or a pseudonym, but she'd been going by that name for well over twenty years as she penned at least one successful lesbian romance per year (in some years, two). I wasn't really a fan of her work—she'd been pretty good when she first got started, but quite frankly it seemed like she'd been phoning it in for years. At some point her publisher started calling her "the goddess of lesbian love and romance"—obviously a play on her name— but she'd never been short on ego. Jerry had forwarded me one of her emails in which she gave detailed instructions on how she was to be treated and referred to all weekend ("I must *always* be introduced as the award-winning goddess of lesbian love and romance Aphrodite Longwell, anything less would be an INSULT to my stature and contributions to lesbian literature") which had made me laugh for a good four or five minutes.

She gave me an air-kiss on both cheeks, putting her hands

on my shoulders. Her nails were lacquered the same shade of green as her eye shadow, and the index fingers had rhinestones embedded in the nails. She was wearing long dangly gold earrings with rhinestones at the bottom that swung with even the slightest motion of her head. She had a strange habit of tilting her head to one side or the other when she was talking or listening that always reminded me of a canary. She had a rather high-pitched breathy voice that was definitely an affectation for public consumption (her actual speaking voice was much sexier, in my opinion—especially when she was groaning in it while I brought her to orgasm).

"So lovely to see you," she whispered in my ear while the other women stayed a respectable distance from us. "It's been far too long. Are you busy later?"

I bit my lower lip. Surely she wasn't suggesting an assignation? "I don't have any plans, no."

"Maybe we can have a drink in the bar." She tilted her head to the left in that birdlike way. "I heard you were the one who found the body." Her eyes narrowed slightly. "Darling, that must have been so awful."

I inhaled sharply. The Aphrodite I knew wasn't really very concerned about other people. She was a bit of a narcissist, to be kind about it, and the rest of us really only existed to her as we related to her. That ridiculous weekend I'd spent with her at that writers' retreat in Santa Barbara was something I'd regretted for years. Now it was just something I remembered as part of my foolish youth—the kind of thing a young lesbian who was desperate to fall in love would do. And yes, I'd been desperate to fall in love. I was still finishing up my PhD then, working on my very first novel, and a writers' retreat with instruction and classes from lesbian writers in Santa Barbara sounded almost too perfect to me. I finished maxing out my credit cards to pay for the trip, and having read some of Aphrodite's books—at that point, she'd only published three or four, I couldn't remember—I was rather excited to meet her. I wasn't interested in writing romance novels—I've always wanted to be a mystery writer—but I admired her work and thought she might be able to give me some advice that would be useful.

Instead I'd wound up spending a weekend in bed with her and heading back east with some scars that took years to heal.

"You didn't know her, did you?"

It was her turn to inhale sharply. The phony smile she usually wore when I saw her appeared. "Leslie MacKenzie is actually a friend of mine."

I was puzzled at first until I remembered that Leslie MacKenzie was the young adult author Antinous had gone after so nastily. "Really?"

Aphrodite nodded, the smile still plastered on her face. "Our kids were in school together. She asked me for some advice about writing, and I helped her with her first book. She's actually quite good, you know—not like most of these poseurs writing queer lit." Her blue eyes flashed angrily. "The bitch got what she deserved." She stepped back from me and glanced at her watch. "Darling, it's almost time for your class. I'll see you in the bar around five?"

Without waiting for me to say yes, she turned on her heel and clacked out of the book room, her entourage trailing along behind her.

Typical.

CHAPTER FIVE

Despite being slightly unnerved by the prospect of having a drink with an ex from a little less than twenty years ago, I managed somehow to suck it up, and my workshop went extremely well.

I am nothing if not a thorough professional.

Of course, I do teach writing and literature for a living. When and if the day ever comes that I can't give a good workshop on creating character, well, that's the day I need to sit down and reevaluate my life and my career.

My class had twenty attendees, including the four I'd met in the coffee shop, who sat in the very front row and took voluminous notes of almost everything I said. I had some fun exercises that were tried and true successes every time I've used them, whether in a writing class or in a workshop. They certainly worked this time. Once the hour and a half was up, several attendees let me know in the most enthusiastic manner that I'd really helped and inspired them as I gathered my materials and shoved them into my shoulder bag. They also asked more questions, and not just about creating characters—

I'd been surprised no one had asked the tired old question about making a living as a writer during the question-and-answer period at the end of the workshop.

I *hate* being asked that question.

Remembering my own horrible experience with Dr. Dixon in college always made me reluctant to come across as anything other than encouraging to my students. Yet at the same time I didn't want to give anyone false hope either. The truth was it was incredibly difficult to make a living as a writer—I kept hearing things, through social media and other places, that the new "do-it-yourself" ebook model was *the* way to get published and maximize your profits. But no one had ever made a convincing case to me about it—all I could go by was what I saw on my own royalty statements and what Mabel shared with me whenever we had one of our boozy late-night phone calls during which we both drank a lot of wine. So I always said that it had always been difficult to make a living solely from writing—every writer dreams of being self-supporting, but lightning struck only a very select few, and there was no rhyme or reason to it. I'd certainly dreamed that I'd hit it big—and the Laura Lassiter mystery novels did very well for me indeed, but certainly not well enough for me to give up my steady paycheck, my health insurance, and all the other perks that came with my job—like retirement. I couldn't see myself ever not writing, but the thought of *having* to write for the rest of my life so I wouldn't have to live on cat food wasn't exactly a pleasant one.

My writing career could dry up tomorrow.

But you don't want to say that to eager students.

So I'd come up with a standard shtick: *Well, obviously it takes hard work and dedication to be a writer. But to make a living also requires, unfortunately, a lot of luck and being in the right place at the right time with the right book—and that cannot be taught. But I truly believe if you work hard and always do your best, you'll be able to make money writing. It also depends on how well you want to live. I teach because I enjoy it, and I write because I can't imagine* not *writing, and between the two I've put together a really nice life. But if you become a writer because you think you're going to get rich, you're only going to be disappointed in the long run.*

It's a realistic look but not a dream killer at the same time.

I never wanted any student of mine to send me a copy of their first novel with a note like the one I'd sent Dr. Dixon.

Never.

I pulled my shoulder bag on and followed the stragglers out of the room, still answering questions about character creation. "It's always really important to remember that even your nastiest, meanest, most hateful villains—in their own minds they aren't villains," I said as we walked out into the mezzanine lobby. "To the villain, your hero—or heroine—is the villain. Always remember that, and that behavior always comes out of who the character is as a person."

"That's really excellent advice, Winter," a female voice said from behind me.

I stopped and closed my eyes as my stomach turned over and my heart started racing. *Stay calm,* I told myself.

I knew that voice, but it couldn't be.

You knew she'd turn up if you came to New Orleans, Tracy. Isn't that why you really came?

I hate that little voice in my head. It's always right, and it's always smug.

I opened my eyes and forced a smile on my face. I excused myself from my students and turned around. If it was indeed her, I couldn't escape anyway without looking completely insane, and the last thing in the world I wanted to do was make an ass of myself.

Especially in front of my evil ex.

"Dani," I said, managing to keep my tone even and friendly, if not warm. "I was wondering if I'd run into you this weekend."

Just saying her name left a bad taste in my mouth. It was like somehow I'd made the mistake of mixing Italian salad dressing and milk together in my mouth.

My palm itched to slap her face, but I managed to stand there and keep the smile frozen on my face.

She glided across the marble floor toward me with a smile on her beautiful face. I hadn't seen her in person in nearly ten years. Sometimes I had to rip the scab off and watched her on the news with the sound off, and she was still just as beautiful as she was the day I first met her all those years ago. She was almost six feet tall in her bare feet, but she liked to wear what she called "killer heels" and I called torture devices, and today she was wearing a particularly steep pair that made her look absurdly tall. She's always towered over me—and I'm not short at five-eight—Jerry cattily said she used her height to make other people feel inadequate. Jerry had never really cared for her that much, even when we were together. Once we'd gone our separate ways, he gave full rein to his venom. He was actually the one who came up with the term "evil ex" for her.

Today she was wearing a dove-gray skirt that hugged her hips lovingly and a pearl silk blouse. A matching jacket was draped over one of her arms. She looked amazing, if a little too thin—but then she'd always claimed she needed to keep her figure slim for the television cameras. "The camera," she always said, "doesn't add ten pounds—it adds twenty." Her black hair was cut in an asymmetrical wedge that heightened her enormous dark-brown eyes and her perfectly shaped eyebrows. Dani had long ago mastered the art of wearing just enough makeup to flatter her features without overdoing it. Her breasts were still high and firm, even though she was now pushing forty. She put both arms around me, but I just stood there, not responding and not moving. She brushed her cheek against mine and stepped back, that smile still on her face. "You look amazing," she said softly, "like you haven't aged a day since I last saw you." She smelled of some expensive perfume, and I noticed a diamond tennis bracelet draped gracefully around her left wrist.

"You were never a good liar," I replied, amazed that my voice wasn't shaking.

"You do look wonderful." She stepped back and smiled at me a little hesitantly. "Do you have a moment for coffee?" The smile faded and shrank a little bit, the dimples in her cheeks smoothing out a bit. "We haven't talked in forever." She had the decency to blush as she said it.

Not since the night you left me for another woman, I thought. But instead of turning and walking away, I gave a halfhearted shrug. "Beats working on my book."

"A new Laura Lassiter?" Her smile grew and her eyes danced. "How exciting! I've been following your career. I'm so proud of your success, you know. And I didn't know you were writing lesbian romances until I saw it in the paper the other day."

"It was in the paper?" *Damn you, Jerry! That's the only way they could have known.* To be fair, though, I hadn't told him not to tell anyone Winter Lovelace was really Tracy Norris. And he was trying to sell tickets. "I didn't know."

"I'll have to read some of them—I bet they're wonderful."

"Well, they're *fiction*," I replied in a somewhat nastier tone. "After all, a romance novel has to end with a happily-ever-after, and I don't know anything about those, do I?"

That gave her a bit of a pause, but just for a few seconds. Then her on-camera smile was firmly back in place and she gestured for me to follow her down the steps to the hotel's main lobby.

I'm just small enough to admit that I really enjoyed being recognized by several people as we crossed the lobby to the doors to the Carousel Bar, while everyone looked right through Ms. Television News.

She found us a small table for two next to one of the enormous windows looking out onto Royal Street. The Carousel Bar was one of my favorite places in New Orleans to have a drink, and I hadn't had a chance to stop in there yet since checking into the hotel the day before. The round bar rotated in the center of the room—legend had it that it was the old carousel from a long-defunct New Orleans amusement park. The horses had been replaced with ornate chairs anchored firmly in place. I sat down on the banquette with my back to the wall, so she had to take the chair, and let my shoulder bag slide down my arm until it rested on the floor as I took a long look around.

The place had been completely renovated in the years since the last time I'd sat at the rotating bar swilling vodka gimlets with Jerry. With a pang I remembered that was my last night in New Orleans before fleeing to the north shore; Jerry's way of saying good-bye to me was to get me rip-roaringly drunk. I'd had a horrible hangover the next morning as I drove across the lake, I remembered. But the renovation was amazing. The bar had been small before, and very dark in the corners, almost gloomy. Now they'd expanded it so that it took up that entire side of the building, and giant tinted-glass windows looked out onto Royal Street all the way to the corner. *I can't believe I haven't been here in that long,* I thought when a harried-looking waitress came up and smiled at us. "Can I get you something to drink, ladies?"

"I'll just have coffee." Dani turned the full brilliance of her smile onto the young woman, who didn't seem to notice.

"I'll have the same, only put a shot of Baileys in mine," I said when she turned her attention to me.

Dani's eyebrows went up. As soon as the waitress moved away from our table, Dani said, "I don't remember you ever drinking during the day before."

"A lot has changed in ten years," I replied evenly. The tone was sharper than I'd intended, so I added, with what I hoped came across as a carefree shrug, "Besides, I'm done for the day. What's a little Baileys in the afternoon?" I forced a smile on my face and inwardly chastised myself. *Seriously, get over it! It was ten years ago!*

But I wasn't over it, was I?

Over the last ten years, the pain had subsided into a dull ache, and then only on the rare occasions when I was reminded of her or felt the need after too much wine to catch her on the news. But seeing her in person? Sitting across a table from her in a bar? It felt as fresh and new as if it had happened only yesterday. It was taking all of my willpower not to scream "How could you do that to me?" at her.

We were together for a little less than five years.

Daniella Simmons and I had met at a wedding, of all places. The daughter of one of my colleagues in the English department at Tulane, Dr. Melanie O'Connor, was getting married. Melanie's office was next door to mine, and the two of us got along well. On my first day she'd come over with a thermos of coffee to welcome me to the university and had helped me navigate the treacherous waters of the political games played in the department. She was one of the few colleagues of mine there that I actually admired and respected—the majority of them were pompous and pretentious old, straight white men right out of the nineteenth century. Melanie had written and published several amazing critiques of women writers, and *Trashy Books: Best Selling Women's Fiction from 1950–1980* was a text I actually taught in my Modern Fiction course. By the time of the wedding, I still hadn't earned tenure yet but was coming up for review, so attending the wedding—which most of the rest of the department was also attending—would have been a politically and professionally wise move even if I didn't like Melanie and her daughter Nicola. I thought Nicola's fiancé was a bit of a smug fratboy douche in the absolute worst sense of the words. He'd been born to a wealthy family in Ascension Parish and was currently studying for the bar—but he always liked to point out that due to his trust fund, he didn't really need to work. For some reason I couldn't quite fathom, Nicola was crazy about him. I didn't get the impression that Melanie was too fond of him, but she never said anything negative about him…though I always thought I could see her grinding her teeth sometimes when he was talking, which was often.

The man did like the sound of his own voice.

I met Daniella at the reception. I was standing at the dessert table, trying to decide between strawberry cheesecake and a brownie (or both). I was wearing a nice sky-blue Ann Taylor dress I'd found at a lovely consignment shop on Magazine Street—why pay ridiculous prices for designer clothes when you can get almost-new stuff at a fraction of the cost? Besides, what were the odds the original owner of the dress would be at the wedding? It was probably the nicest dress I'd ever owned—I'm not much of a dress wearer, to be honest. I'd also just gotten my long blond hair cut to a manageable shoulder length—I'd decided I was getting a little too old for the ponytail I'd been wearing most of my life. Anyway, I'd just decided to have a slice of the cheesecake *and* the brownie when she came strolling up in a pair of black slingback stilettos. I was a little awed by the ease with which she navigated through the grass in those heels—I always wore flats, never mastered the art of wearing shoes with heels no matter how hard my mother had tried to teach me. Dani was wearing a gorgeous gold skirt and jacket suit with a pale-blue silk blouse, and her dark hair curled and fell around her face in ways I'd prayed my straight blond hair would when I was a little girl. She was quite beautiful, and my most recent relationship had just ended, having lasted a whole whopping three weeks from start to finish. She started flirting with me and I responded—and she wound up going home with me after the reception ended. She was a senior at LSU School of Journalism and had interned at one of the local New Orleans stations that summer...and was hopeful they would hire her once she had her diploma in hand.

As I was about to learn, Dani Simmons always got what she wanted.

And didn't care what she had to do to get it.

It seemed like the next thing I knew, we were a happy couple with an amazing sex life, who had amazing conversations about literature and pop culture. I let her read my first novel in manuscript form—my agent was looking for a publisher at that point, and when I landed a deal with one of the major houses in New York, it was Dani I celebrated with. She drove down from Baton Rouge every Friday afternoon to stay at my little house above Claiborne and woke up before dawn every Monday to drive back for her first class. And once she had her diploma and a job at the local ABC affiliate, she moved in with me. It was a good time—I'd just gotten tenure, the first Laura Lassiter novel had been released to critical acclaim and terrific sales. For the next few years everything was great—it seemed like I'd found my happily-ever-after. I had a great job, I had a great burgeoning career as a mystery writer, and I was madly, hopelessly in love. My parents adored Dani, and so did my older brother. We even were talking about having a child—either adopting or getting a sperm donor.

I, of course, would have carried the child had we gone the sperm donor route. Dani was always worried about her figure. If I'd heard that tired old trope about the camera adding weight once, I'd heard it a million times.

And then in just under a year, everything about my wonderful, happy life went straight to hell.

My parents were killed in a car accident. They'd rented a condo on the beach in the Florida panhandle for a couple of weeks, and on their way home the driver of an eighteen-wheeler fell asleep at the wheel. They had called me before they started on their way. They'd been wonderful parents, loving and supportive of my brother and me. They never cared that I was lesbian—I was their daughter first and foremost, and my happiness had always been paramount in their minds. Their car was mangled and smashed so completely there was no question they might have survived.

The funeral was closed casket.

That was bad enough, but the Fates weren't finished with me just yet.

My older brother Clay, a sculptor, had moved to the north shore after splitting with his wife about the time I met Dani. The split was amicable, and Celia was still a friend of the family— but she'd remarried and moved away to Houston when her second husband was transferred. About three months after our parents were killed, Clay was diagnosed with cancer. Taking care of Clay fell squarely on my shoulders. I was still reeling from the loss of my parents, and the thought of losing my last living relative was more than I could imagine. I found myself spending more and more time on the north shore, and less and less time with Dani. Sometimes it seemed like we went days without seeing each other. Even when I was in New Orleans, I was so horribly depressed and upset that I pushed her away. I'd never been good with sharing my grief; I preferred to deal with it myself. I hated burdening other people with my drama.

Unfortunately, Dani was the kind of woman who needed attention, and a lot of it. I was just a big bundle of misery, still in mourning for my parents, horrified I was going to lose my brother—the cancer was spreading really fast—and trying to keep my classes under control while writing yet another book. I just didn't have time for Dani—and in the years since I caught her cheating on me, I have gradually began taking ownership of my own part in what happened. I shut her out, trying too hard to deal with everything on my own, trying to be strong and not burden her with my problems. I'd come to realize through three-times-a-week sessions with a therapist that it had been a huge mistake. I'd pushed her away, closed her out, and couldn't place all of the blame on her the way I so passionately wanted to. I found out about her affair shortly before Clay died, and I was in no place to have a rational conversation or to try to salvage anything from the wreckage of my relationship. I threw her out, wouldn't listen to her, wouldn't talk to her—there was nothing she could possibly have to say that I wanted to hear. And when Clay passed away, I chucked my entire life in New Orleans. He'd left his gorgeous house in Rouen to me, and I sold the little house in New Orleans I'd loved so much and moved away. I resigned from Tulane once I landed a tenured position at the University of Louisiana-Rouen, leaving New Orleans for good and never looking back.

And that was when I started writing lesbian romances in addition to the mystery series. That way I wouldn't have time to dwell on anything that happened to me, how my life had suddenly gone off the rails or how alone I was. I didn't want to look back, and by focusing on my students and my writing, I didn't have the time anyway.

Occasionally, in a moment of self-awareness, it would occur to me that I wrote the romances to satisfy my own emotional needs. It was a way of experiencing love and romance without actually risking the emotional damage that can come with the real thing. I made some friends on the faculty and of some of my neighbors, but for the most part I kept to myself, always saying I had to work, and avoided any emotional entanglements.

Every once in a while, late at night when I was finished writing or grading papers or had finished reading a book, I felt lonely. The house was pretty big, and sometimes it could feel really empty. The cats helped some, but cuddling with them wasn't always enough to make the ache go away for good.

Mabel, my agent, often told me it wasn't the healthiest way to live, but it worked for me. And why mess with something that works?

"I appreciated the flowers," Dani said after our waitress dropped off our drinks. She sipped at her coffee. "That was kind of you."

"Yeah, well, I'm not that big a bitch," I replied, stirring sweetener into my coffee. "And I got your thank-you card."

Mary Digby, the woman she'd left me for, died last summer. I didn't even know she'd been sick; Jerry had emailed me after she died.

"You know, I'm sorry about how all of that played out," Dani said quietly, nervously twisting a lock of hair around her index finger. She always did that when she was uncomfortable and nervous. "I treated you like shit and—"

"It was ten years ago." I interrupted her. "All water under the bridge now. We were younger, things didn't work out, it got ugly. I got over it. It's okay, Dani. I appreciate your apology, but I really don't want to hash this all out now."

It wasn't entirely true, but I also knew what I wanted—her to get on her knees, weep and wail and pound on her chest as she begged me for forgiveness—wasn't going to happen.

I never said I was a good person.

And she'd suffered enough, hadn't she? I didn't know what had killed Mary, but that horrible year of death and dying I'd experienced was something I would never want anyone else to go through. I wouldn't wish that on someone I hated.

And no matter how much I tried, I couldn't hate Dani.

And I also figured, hey—if there ever was a good time for someone to cheat on me and leave me for someone else, it was when all of my emotions and feelings were muted and numbed by the deaths of everyone in my immediate family.

I reached across the table and patted her hand gently. "I am really sorry about Mary."

She wiped at her eyes and gave me a brave smile. "Thanks. That means a lot. I'd like for us to be friends again at least. I've missed you."

Let's not get carried away here. I took a deep breath and asked her about her career, to change the subject. Dani always did like to talk about herself—and apparently widowhood hadn't changed that.

As she talked about station politics and her hopes for getting an anchor position on the early-morning news show, I looked past her and saw the young man from the book room sitting at the slowly rotating bar. He was shoveling appetizers into his mouth and nursing what looked like a Coke. As I watched, that publisher Jerry hated so much walked up and sat down at the bar next to him, and they started talking.

Now, isn't that interesting? Dani was still talking, and the sound of the massive televisions and other people talking created a wall of sound so I couldn't hear anything they were saying to each other.

One thing I'd noticed in the past at writers' conferences or fan conferences was that writers liked to drink. Writers liked to drink a lot. I took a sip of my coffee and regretted ordering it almost immediately. Even though the air-conditioning was turned down to meat locker-levels, the air was still a bit heavy and the coffee was too hot.

"Your class was wonderful." The woman from the coffee shop—the one with the dark pigtails—was standing there next to our table, fidgeting.

"Thank you," I replied, trying to remember her name. Pat or Demi? Which one was she? I am terrible with names, and the lanyard with her name tag in it wasn't around her neck. "I'm glad you enjoyed it."

"I was wondering if I could speak with you?" she asked

again, looking down and her face flushing a bit. "It won't take long. Just a minute of your time?" There was a pleading note in her voice.

Demi, I remembered, *Pat was the other one.* I gave Dani an inquiring look.

She just sighed and waved her hand slightly. "Far be it from me to keep you from your adoring fans." She sounded tired and maybe a little disappointed.

But that was probably just wishful thinking on my part.

"I won't be long," I assured her, and followed Demi out of the bar to a secluded couch near the entrance to the restaurant.

"I'm so sorry to bother you," she said hurriedly, her eyes darting around the lobby like she was afraid someone might overhear us. "But I have to talk to someone."

"What's the matter?" I asked, mystified.

"I can't talk to my friends, they wouldn't understand," she said hurriedly, her eyes still darting around.

Her behavior was making me nervous, frankly. "What wouldn't they understand?"

"I don't know, maybe it's a mistake to talk to you."

She was beginning to get on my nerves. I stood up. "Well, if that's the case I'll get back to my friend."

"No, please!" She grabbed my arm and squeezed it pretty hard. I winced, and she loosened her grip without letting go. "I'm sorry, I just don't know what to do."

I sat back down. "Well, why don't you just go ahead and tell me what it is. I'll help you if I can."

"Thank you." She let go of my hand and reached into her purse. She pulled out an envelope, which she looked at for a moment before looking at me, then back to the envelope. "I can't tell my friends, you understand," she half whispered, looking around again before leaning in toward me and lowering her voice yet again, so I could barely hear her over the noise in the lobby. "They wouldn't understand. But..." She bit her lower lip.

"Spit it out," I said sharply. I was getting really annoyed now.

"I'm staying at the Maintenon, and I was looking out my window, you know, right about the time she fell, and I was taking pictures, you know, of the view and things...and I caught something in the pictures..." Her voice trailed off.

I didn't have to ask whose room, of course. "Did you tell the police? You need to tell the police."

"I couldn't." She started trembling again, and she looked over my shoulder. Her eyes widened, and her face paled. "Oh no!" She tossed the envelope into my lap and ran, her flip-flops slapping against the marble lobby floor.

What the hell? I turned to look over my shoulder in the direction she'd been looking and saw Kyle Bennett standing by a table in the restaurant, talking to a man with his back to me.

Why did seeing him spook her so much?

I sighed and shoved the envelope into my pocket before walking back into the bar. I slid back into my seat and took a big gulp of my now-tepid coffee. "Sorry."

"What was that about?" Dani's coffee cup was practically empty. She gave me a crooked smile. "I didn't think you were going to come back, really." She lowered her eyes. "Not that I can blame you, after what I did to you."

"You don't have to wear sackcloth and ashes," I retorted sharply. "Snap out of it, Dani. It's okay, really." I put my hand on top of hers. "It is nice to see you again, you know. I thought about calling—to offer my condolences…after she died, but then I thought…"

"You're a good person—that's more than I deserve from you." Dani smiled at me, wiping at her eyes. It was amazing how her makeup never ran or smeared, no matter what she did to it.

"Well, I like to think I'm a good person." I looked over to where Demi's friends had been sitting. The table was empty. I frowned. "But really…" I took a deep breath and realized how nice it was to be sitting with her, without rancor or anger.

It *had* been ten years.

Dani followed my glance and gave me a questioning look.

"Do you know who's investigating the death yesterday? The one I witnessed?" I turned back to her. She worked for a television station news division; odds were pretty good she had a good idea what was going on. I opened my backpack and fished through my wallet for the card the pompous asshole detective had given me yesterday. I found it, crumpled in the change pocket, and smoothed it out. "This Al Randisi guy?"

"Randisi?" She made a face. "I've had to interview him before. He's a pain in the ass, frankly, to interview. He hates reporters and doesn't go out of his way to hide it. Why?"

"That woman—Demi—I don't know her last name. I think he should probably talk to her." I started to mention the envelope she'd tossed in my lap, but changed my mind. It was probably nothing. *I'll open it later, when I'm alone,* I decided. "It was really weird. She started to tell me something, but then she got spooked and ran out." I unlocked my phone but frowned at the card.

What exactly was I going to say to Randisi? That a woman

whose last name I didn't know might know something about Antinous Renault's death?

Jerry would know her last name.

I opened the contacts app, found Jerry's name, and sent him a text: *Do you know the last name of a woman in my workshop whose first name is Demi?* I put the phone back down on the table as I noticed Aphrodite and her entourage walking into the bar. She waved at me, and she and her little group sat down at the table where Demi and her friends had been sitting.

I smiled at Dani. "I hate to cut this short, but I kind of made plans to meet someone for a drink, and she's here. This was really nice."

Dani glanced over at Aphrodite's group. "Are you going to be at the party later?"

I nodded as I stood. "The opening reception? Yes, I'll be there."

"Okay." Dani touched my hand, delicately tracing her fingertips along the top of it. "Maybe we can talk some more?"

"I'd like that." Impulsively I leaned over and kissed her cheek. "Thanks for the drink."

CHAPTER SIX

I saw Dani walk out of the bar as I slid into the booth across from where Aphrodite was sitting.

"Tracy, this is Marty Winthrop and Brenna Abbott," she said, nodding to each woman in turn, "and ladies, this is Tracy Norris, who writes the Laura Lassiter novels *and* lesbian romance as Winter Lovelace."

"I'm a huge fan," the woman on my side of the booth, Marty Winthrop, said, shaking my hand vigorously. She was a butch, wearing a ribbed white tank top and a pair of faded 501 Levi's with holes at the knees. Her dark hair was cut into wings that feathered back on the sides and was left long in the back. She had a barbed-wire tattoo around her muscular right biceps, and I could see a dolphin tattoo on her right shoulder blade. "I love Laura Lassiter, but I can't help but think she just needs to come out of the closet and settle down with the right woman!"

I laughed. "If I had a dollar for every time I've heard that, I'd own an island in the Caribbean and could retire."

"We wouldn't want that!" Brenna Abbott smiled at me from across the table. She was a pretty redhead with almond-shaped green eyes and a heart-shaped face. Her red hair was cut into a cute bob that flattered the shape of her face. "I have to confess I haven't read your romances."

"And if I had a dollar for every time I've heard that…" I let my voice trail off and they all laughed.

I ordered a vodka tonic and allowed myself to relax. I've always had problems dealing with exes. I wasn't sure why, to be honest—I just always felt rather uncomfortable around them. Jerry told me once it was because I hated failure more than anything else, and my exes were a reminder that I'd failed at something. There might be some truth to that. I did hate failing, but I wasn't the only person who'd failed at relationships—given the divorce rate for straight people, and I didn't exactly know a lot of long-term queer couples. Jerry, as far as I could remember, had never really had anything that could remotely be considered a relationship; he always said he wasn't interested in having one. I couldn't help but wonder, though, if he actually felt that way or if that was simply his way of accepting that he didn't have one?

Although I also couldn't be completely sure what it said about *me* that I was going from sitting with one ex to sitting with another. Was a weekend with someone enough to give them ex status? I wasn't sure, but I'd always counted Aphrodite as one. As I looked across the table at her smiling at me, I wondered how she remembered our weekend together at that conference.

The sex had been pretty terrific, as I recalled. But we hadn't even tried to make anything out of it. We both went our separate ways afterward, I back to New Orleans and she back to Seattle. We hadn't even stayed in touch via email and had been icily polite to each other on those rare occasions we'd been in the same place again. Jerry couldn't stand her, but had never said why and waved away any questions.

I smiled back at her. The waitress set my drink down in front of me, and Aphrodite told her to add it to her tab. I toasted her with my glass, and then Brenna asked while I was taking a sip, "So, you really didn't know Antinous Renault before this weekend?"

I almost choked on my drink—which was much stronger than it had any right to be. I managed to get it down and replied, after taking a deep breath, "No. I met her at the airport in Atlanta yesterday—we were on the same flight here. I'd never even heard of her before that." I gave a slight shrug. "I'm not really as up on things in queer publishing as maybe I should be."

"Well, you mostly write in the mainstream," Marty replied. "And this little world is so incestuous and—well, it can be kind of a snake pit."

I nodded, but didn't look at Aphrodite. "What was your experience with her?" I looked at Marty, whose face was flushed.

"She's gone after me a few times," Marty admitted with a shake of her head. "But nothing ever really came of it. It's not like anyone who read her blog or her website was likely to read anything I write anyway. They're all about objectifying gay men." She said the last with a sneer. "Because, you know, gay men are there for their pleasure. She sickened me. She was the worst of them." She drummed her fingers on the table. "It's at the very least cultural appropriation. Imagine if white people were writing highly sexualized novels about people of color. It's the same thing."

"You're generalizing," Brenna pointed out. "You know

some of the straight women who write this stuff actually do care about actual gay men—"

"How is it any different than fucking *Penthouse Letters*?" Marty demanded. "Or those ridiculous porn movies where women fuck other women for the titillation of straight men? As both a lesbian and a feminist, that's revolting. So how is it any different when straight women do the same thing to gay men?"

"But gay porn is made for gay men," Aphrodite interjected, "not for straight women." She shrugged. "I personally watch gay porn. It's really hot. Does that mean that I'm a bad feminist, or that I'm objectifying gay men? Does that mean as a feminist I'm a hypocrite?"

"One could," I said slowly, "make the argument that women have been objectified and sexualized and oppressed for millennia, so the objectification of men by women is simply a little payback?"

"So two wrongs would make a right?" Marty asked.

"I'm also not sure that it's okay to tell someone they can't write what they want to, what they are passionate about." Brenna took a sip of her drink. "I don't want anyone telling me what I can or cannot write, so how can I tell other writers they can't write something?"

"It's kind of a slippery slope," I said. "I haven't really thought about any of this, honestly—I'd never heard of this 'm/m' stuff before this weekend, but I'm kind of with Brenna. Telling someone they can't write about something seems an awful lot like censorship to me." I shrugged. Under the table Marty's knee brushed against mine, but I ignored it. It was probably accidental. "It seems like this is all a question of morality, a philosophical argument. If we believe in freedom of speech, and freedom of thought, then every writer is free to write about what they want to, whatever they're passionate about. No writer, of course, has the right to be published, and no writer has a right to an audience."

"All well and good," Aphrodite replied, "but then the question becomes, so does a straight woman have the right to set herself up as the definitive authority on what is or isn't gay male fiction, what should and shouldn't be written?"

"I would say no." I leaned across the table. "Unless someone has actually known the actual societal oppression that a gay man has faced—then she doesn't have the right or authority to talk about what is or isn't authentic." I picked up my drink and stared at the melting ice before taking another drink. "Of course, she has every right to discuss whether or not the story works, whether the writing is good or if it isn't— since all of that is subjective in the first place. But to determine whether it's authentic, and pretend like you're some kind of expert? She just needs to shut the fuck up. On the other hand, I do believe that a woman—any woman, regardless of her sexuality—can understand and relate to the oppression faced by gay men because women are historically an oppressed class." I exhaled. "This is some pretty heavy discussion for cocktail hour!"

They all laughed, and Marty's knee brushed against mine again. I glanced at her, but she wasn't looking at me. *Calm down,* I told myself. *You're sitting on the same side of the table. She's not making a move on you. You're getting a buzz from the liquor. You should slow it down.*

"Regardless of whatever our opinions may or may not be," Aphrodite said finally, "I think we can all agree that Antinous was a terrible person. What she did to Leslie..." She shook her head. "It was really unforgivable, especially when you consider what a fucking phony she was herself."

"You actually saw her fall?" Brenna asked me.

I shook my head and started to take another drink, but put the glass back down. Yes, I was starting to get a bit of a buzz, and the opening reception was starting in about another half hour—which meant more alcohol. I had long ago realized that I was, if not an alcoholic, a *compulsive* social drinker. I generally have a glass or two of wine at night before I go to bed—if even that. I never feel like I need to have a drink, or actively go out looking to get drunk. My problem is I have a bit of social anxiety, and at parties, I tend to start drinking and continue drinking until I get stumbling, falling-down drunk. This is kind of embarrassing—and I've been assured any number of times by enough different people for me to believe it's true—that I never seem drunk or do or say something I shouldn't.

Hardly reassuring, though, when you wake up with your head feeling like someone's buried a hatchet in the center of your forehead and the previous evening is nothing more than a blur.

"No, I didn't," I replied, wondering how many times I was going to have to tell this story over the weekend. "I was sitting underneath the gallery. She landed in front of me. I didn't see her go over the railing, or even if she was alone up there."

I saw someone go into her room, I heard Demi saying again in my head. I decided to find her at the opening party and ask her some pointed questions about what she'd seen.

Surely she'd be there.

"You think someone killed her?" This was from Marty, in a hushed voice, and I came out of my reverie to realize they were all staring at me.

"Well, if she was trying to kill herself, it was a weird way to do it, don't you think?" I countered. "And I doubt very seriously she went over the railing by accident." And she *had* gone over the railing, I realized. Had she fallen through it, I would have heard the wood splinter and break, and there would have been pieces of the wooden railing scattered around her body.

It *was* murder.

I'd sort of witnessed a murder.

Yeah, you're a genius, aren't you? You should write mysteries!

I bit my lower lip as Aphrodite waved the waitress over and signed for the tab. There was some talk, discussion about going to the opening reception, and I heard myself agreeing to walk over with them.

My mind was still wrapping itself around my realization that Antinous had been murdered. *Why did it take me so long to figure this out? Did I just not want to accept it?* Maybe it was just a delayed reaction?

Hadn't I told Jerry last night at dinner it had to be murder?

But that had been more of an intellectual exercise, which must have been a way of pushing back against the reality.

I followed them out of the hotel, and we walked up Royal Street. The opening reception was being held at a historic home on St. Peter Street, a few blocks away. As we walked, I was aware that the conversation was continuing around me, but my mind wasn't in it. Aphrodite and Brenna were walking slightly ahead of Marty and me, but I wasn't participating—I was trying to remember exactly the sequence of events. I had heard the door above me open, and then noises—the groaning of weakened wood as weight was put on it. I hadn't heard footsteps, which was also odd—but if someone had tossed her body over the railing, they could have walked away quickly and I wouldn't have heard anything because I was too busy screaming.

I saw him go into her room.

I kept hearing Demi's voice in my head and remembering the look on her face as she looked past me in the lobby of the Monteleone.

It *had* been terror I'd seen on her face, hadn't it? She'd seen someone or something that scared her out of talking to me, and she'd taken off like a bat out of hell.

The envelope. She gave me an envelope.

I shoved my hand into my pocket and felt it there. I'd just shoved it into my pocket and completely forgotten about it because I was so wrapped up in my goddamned Dani drama.

This is why I am NOT Jessica Fletcher.

I pulled the envelope out. There was something in it. I tore open the end and dumped whatever it was into my hand.

It was a flash drive made to look like a small magnifying glass. I pulled the end off, and there was the thingy you'd stick into a USB port.

But why would Demi give this to *me*?

I put it back in my pocket. I definitely needed to find her at the party.

I was feeling overheated—a combination of the alcohol and the humidity—by the time we reached the historic Gaspard Metoyer house. There was a volunteer with a name badge hanging around his neck standing in the entryway at the top of the stairs. "Welcome." He smiled as he opened the front door and waved us inside. "There's no smoking inside the house or on the grounds, and all food and drink has to remain outside in the courtyard. There are several bars set up, and the food buffet is on the far side of the courtyard. Enjoy yourselves."

The Gaspard Metoyer house was one of the oldest houses in the French Quarter. I'd always been aware it existed but had never actually been inside before. A young woman introduced herself and offered to give us a tour of the house, should we want one. I smiled at her as I declined, glad she was dressed like a professional businesswoman and not in period drag. Period drag always annoyed me, reminding me that when people dressed like that they also owned slaves, which they often glossed over in the overdone Southern belle accents as they played Scarlett O'Hara and tried to make it seem like the antebellum South was this wonderful land of gentlemen and ladies. Aphrodite, Brenna, and Marty, however, opted for a tour and followed the young woman down a side hallway as I made my way toward the back gallery, where I could hear the hubbub of a party.

The gallery was completely enclosed in glass, and the beauty of the courtyard made me catch my breath. The house extended back on either side of the courtyard, giving the house a large U shape. There was a tall stone fence at the rear of the courtyard, and I could see the back of another house on its other side. The two back wings had upper galleries, but on the courtyard level there weren't doors—just enormous openings into big rooms that I could tell were where the slaves had done their laboring for their Metoyer masters in times past. The courtyard itself was huge. There were two gigantic fountains with brass statues of nymphs at the front, and I could see two others at the far end. The courtyard itself was divided into three separate walkways past the fountains, with two long hedges trimmed to about three feet tall serving as dividers. I could see bars set up in several different places with small groups in front of each, as well as other groups talking and milling about scattered throughout the place. At the very end of the center path were several enormous tables sagging under the weight of the food piled high on top of them. Waitpersons wearing black bowties, black slacks, and white shirts circulated amongst the groups of people carrying silver trays with hors d'oeuvres on them. I slowly made my way to the bottom of the back steps and noticed Demi's friends standing off to one side—but Demi wasn't with them.

"Hi," I said, walking up to them and giving them my friendliest smile. They were all holding paper plates in one hand and there were clear, full plastic cups on the flagstones at their feet. "How's the food?"

Mike finished chewing something and swallowed. "The bacon-wrapped shrimp is amazing. I also like the remoulade."

"I'm not sure what kind of spread this is," Pat gestured to some crackers on her plate piled high with some orange-colored paste, "and it looks nasty, but it is fucking delicious. I could make a meal out of it."

"It's all pretty good," Travis chimed in. "I'd stay away from the red wine, though. It's almost vinegar."

"Great, I'll keep that in mind," I replied. "Where's your friend? Demi?"

Pat shrugged. "You were the last to see her."

"Oh?"

"Yeah, she left the bar with you and that was the last we saw of her." Mike replied before popping another bacon-wrapped shrimp in his mouth. "Did she say anything to you? We knocked on her room door before we came to the party, but there was no answer."

"She was supposed to come here with us." Pat sounded more than a little annoyed. "But she's not answering her phone or responding to texts. We have reservations at Bayona for eight, so hopefully she'll just show up there."

"Has she been acting weird?" I asked, trying to keep my tone casual.

"She has seemed a little quiet." Mike knelt down and took a drink from his cup. "Since yesterday."

"Yeah." Pat nodded. "Ever since, well, you know." She made a face. "Demi hated that woman just as much as the rest of us, though. I don't know why it would upset her. I just figured she was tired or something."

"Are you all staying at the Maintenon?"

They all nodded, and Travis said, "Yeah, we're all on upper floors. I have a little balcony on Dauphine Street, so I don't have to go anywhere to smoke." He sighed. "The last time I was in New Orleans, you could pretty much smoke anywhere."

"You need to just quit," Mike replied, getting a scowl in response.

They started bickering about smoking, but I asked Pat where exactly Demi's room was.

"She's at the end of the third floor." Pat frowned at me. "She has a little balcony that looks down on the pool. Why do you ask?"

"Just curious." I shrugged. "You don't think she saw what happened to Antinous, do you?"

"She would have said something to me." Pat dismissed it with a wave of her free hand.

"Okay, well, can you tell her that I'm looking for her?" I gave her a false smile. "I was really enjoying our conversation, but it got cut off and I'd like to talk to her some more."

Pat nodded, and I moved down the center path to the back where the food tables were. I didn't recognize any of the people milling about filling plates, so I grabbed one and loaded up with the bacon-wrapped shrimp and some shrimp remoulade. I added some pasta salad, made my way to a secluded corner of the courtyard, and sat down.

No sooner had I popped one of the bacon-wrapped shrimp in my mouth (and Mike was right—it was delicious and the shrimp practically melted on my tongue) than Jerry plopped down beside me and offered me a plastic cup of fizzy white wine. I took it from him and had a sip to wash the food down.

"Prosecco?" I said once I'd swallowed. "You're serving prosecco?"

"Bitch, please." He waived his hand, crossing his legs at the ankle and leaning back in the chair. "I brought that for me—everyone else can have the shit wine I got donated." He grinned at me. "I've heard great things about your workshop."

"Thanks," I replied. The prosecco was delicious—I might have known Jerry wouldn't drink anything cheap. "This food is good."

He nodded. "Thanks. It was a bitch getting it donated." He sighed. "I'll be so glad when this fucking weekend is over—I just finished talking to that detective, Randisi, again. Why they couldn't have assigned someone not homophobic to the case is a mystery for the ages." He rubbed his forehead. "She was definitely murdered, you were right about that."

"Did he tell you anything else?"

"She was hit over the head with a blunt instrument—blunt force trauma. Then whoever killed her tossed her over the railing, I guess in an attempt to make it look like suicide." He rolled his eyes. "Obviously an amateur—you figured it out last night yourself."

I frowned. "But really, that doesn't make any sense, Jerry.

She was heavy. It wouldn't have been easy for someone to lift all that dead weight over the railing."

He flexed his biceps. "I could have done it, I guess—that's what Randisi was implying, at any rate." He scowled. "I didn't like her either—but I wasn't about to kill her."

"Why did you invite her?" I finished the prosecco and felt my buzz coming back again. "Given everything you said about her, and everything I've heard about her, why on earth would you include her in the program?"

"It was mean," Jerry replied, having the decency to color slightly. "She had no idea how much I hated her, of course—for some reason she got it in her head that I liked her, if you can believe that, because one time I posted on a message board somewhere that writers could write whatever they wanted." He scowled again. "For some reason, that made her think that I was a hundred percent behind her. I wasn't. I hated her. I hated what she did on her blog and her website. And then when she was exposed…" He inhaled. "I sent her an invitation. I didn't think she'd actually have the nerve to show up, but she did. I couldn't believe she accepted…so as soon as she did, I of course invited Anne Howard and Leslie MacKenzie." He sighed. "I seriously didn't think anyone would kill her…I just feel bad for Anne and Leslie. They're staying at the Maintenon, too, you know. It doesn't look good for either one of them."

"Are they here?"

"That's Leslie at the food table." He nodded in that direction. "You want to meet her?"

I nodded and followed him over to the table.

Leslie MacKenzie was small—that was the first thing I noticed about her, and whenever I'd thought of her since then all I could think about was how small she was. She couldn't have been taller than five feet, and she couldn't have weighed more than ninety pounds on a fat day. She had salt-and-pepper hair cut very short. She was wearing a pair of khaki shorts that she was swimming in, and a black T-shirt with *I Love My Gay Son* written across the front in gold glitter. The most dominant feature in her face was her eyes—they were enormous and a vibrant, warm dark brown. She wasn't wearing much makeup, and there were wrinkles at the corners of her eyes and mouth. She could have been any age from thirty-five to sixty. "It's lovely to meet you," she said once Jerry had introduced us. "This is my son, Lance."

Lance was the very large man standing on her other side, who just smiled and mumbled something and went back to focusing on his food. He was at least six foot four, and he had the thickly muscled body of a football player. His dark hair was a little long, and he'd slicked it up into a fauxhawk in the center of his head. He was wearing gravity-defying baggy jeans that hung from his hips and a white oversized Lady Gaga T-shirt. There were some pimples scattered loosely over his tanned skin, and like his mother, he had enormous brown eyes. There was a tattoo of an ankh on his forearm.

Jerry excused himself and disappeared back into the crowd as Leslie looked at me a little more sharply. "You're the one who found the body, aren't you?"

I might as well resign myself to being identified that way all weekend, I thought as I said out loud, "Yes, I did. She landed just a few feet from where I was sitting."

"That must have been traumatizing," she commiserated, putting her right hand on my arm. "You poor thing."

"It was good enough for her," Lance rumbled in a deep baritone voice. "The bitch had it coming."

"Lance!" Leslie snapped.

"Sorry," he mumbled to me, lowering his eyes and going back to piling enough food on his plate to feed a small village.

She clicked her tongue and shook her head at me. "I didn't raise him to talk about women that way, you know. But—" She sighed. "When it comes to that woman—God rest her soul—I guess I shouldn't be surprised at anything anyone says, really. I know you're not supposed to speak ill of the dead, but…"

"I heard she targeted you and your son? That must have been dreadful."

Lance scowled, took his plate, and walked away from us.

"He's just a kid, for all his size," Leslie observed. "Let's sit down and talk while we eat?" She turned and looked at where Lance had sat down and was wolfing his food down like he'd not eaten in weeks. She sighed and allowed me to lead her to where I'd been sitting. She put her plate on her lap once she was seated. "He's only nineteen, you see. He came out to me when he was thirteen. He was so terrified we'd reject him." She clicked her tongue again. "You hear about it all the time, of course, parents rejecting their gay children. How any parent can stop loving their child is beyond me." She looked at me. "Was that your experience?"

"No." I smiled. "I came out to my parents when I was thirteen, but I wasn't worried about it. My parents were very liberal, and it didn't faze or bother them in the least. My older brother was gay."

"Was?"

"He died about ten years ago."

"I'm sorry!"

"It's okay." I smiled back at her. "I still miss him, of course, but I've come to terms with the loss. Time does help."

"Yes, it does, but it never really makes up for that empty

feeling, does it?" She said softly. "Lance was actually a twin. His brother died shortly after he was born. I always wonder what Marlon would have been like…you never get over it." She broke off suddenly. "But it was horrible what that woman did, you know." She shook her head. "I didn't mind—when you're an author, you have to expect to be attacked and have horrible things said about your work."

"It doesn't make it any easier," I replied. "I can still remember my first bad review—word for word."

"Really?" She looked startled. "I suppose that's one way of dealing with it, but me? I just put that kind of thing out of my head. Acknowledge and move on, that's always been my motto. But attacking me through my child was pretty low, even for someone as despicable as Antinous." Her eyes glittered. "Yes, it really did upset me when it happened at first. I cried—the bitch actually made me cry." She laughed. "Listen to me! I guess I'm not as over it as I thought. But I did put it out of my head, and that would have been the end of it. But Antinous wasn't the kind of person who liked to be ignored, you know? She did everything for attention, really. Such a sad person, if you think about it. I've never understood the mentality that any attention was better than no attention, have you?"

"I've known any number of people like that," I replied. "And no, I can never figure it out either. But then I don't really go out of my way seeking attention."

Liar. If you didn't want attention you wouldn't publish, now would you?

"I don't know how Lance found out about it. But he did." She closed her eyes. "He was horribly upset—his father and I have been divorced now for almost ten years, and his father isn't very involved—he's followed me up with a couple of trophy wives he trades in when they age out—and Lance got into it with her online a few times, that's how Anne Howard got involved."

"She's the one who outed Antinous as a woman, right?"

Leslie nodded. "I've never met her—Anne, I mean—but we've corresponded briefly." She gave me a sad smile. "Somehow, Anne found out that Antinous and Lance were fighting online—and there was already some bad blood there. They used to be friends, from what I gathered, and then they had a massive falling-out of some kind. Anyway, they had this feud going—and Anne hired a private detective to find out whatever he could about Antinous. He was the one who found out about the model she'd been using for public appearances, and so forth, and just sat on the information, waiting for her to do something else. When Anne found out about her coming after me and Lance, that was it—she exposed her to the entire world." She shrugged. "I don't know what she hoped to gain from it, but it certainly didn't run her out of publishing, did it?"

No, but someone made sure she was finished.

CHAPTER SEVEN

I woke up Saturday morning with a slight headache and a severe case of cottonmouth, but that wasn't the worst part.

That would be the fact that I wasn't alone in my bed.

It might have been ten years, but I'd recognize those distinctive snores anywhere.

Dani.

I had a vague memory of staggering back to the hotel with her. I moaned to myself. *Great, this is just exactly what you need. You finally come to terms with everything that happened in the past, and now this? This is a complication you do not need, Tracy. How could you have been so stupid?*

Prosecco, that's how.

This is a prime example of why I don't get drunk at parties anymore.

Carefully, I pushed the covers back and slipped out of the bed without waking her. She'd always slept like the dead—I used to tease her that she could sleep through a nuclear holocaust, and that had obviously not changed. I had a vague memory that she'd been too drunk to drive when we'd finally decided to call it a night, and the prosecco had loosened me up enough to invite her to spend the night rather than telling her to call a goddamned cab and pick up her car in the morning.

I shut the bathroom door behind me carefully, so it didn't make any noise, and got a cup of coffee started in the Keurig. It brewed while I brushed my teeth and washed my face. I rinsed my mouth out a few times, then brushed again. It felt like my teeth and tongue had grown fur during the night, and my sinuses were achy despite the arctic temperature in the hotel. I took my vitamins and a Claritin and washed my face yet again as the cobwebs started clearing out of my idiot head.

Stupid, stupid, stupid—you're way too old to be acting like a teenager in heat, I chided my reflection in the mirror. It wasn't pretty. My hair looked like a rat's nest, and my eyes were so red and puffy I could probably frighten small children. They also ached a bit, and I gulped down some aspirin to try to make everything stop hurting.

As I stared at my scary reflection, more vague memories from last night flashed through my mind like a montage from some bad romantic comedy—all that was missing was a sappy power ballad from a once-popular hard rock band. I remembered kissing her in the elevator and pushing her up against the wall, my leg going in between hers while I stroked her breasts. She hadn't resisted. In fact, I could feel her heat on my leg as her arms went around to pull me closer into her, her hands cupping my butt and pulling me tighter against her. Then the elevator stopped at my floor and we'd separated, smiling at each other. I remembered being so turned on the hall seemed endless, like we would never get to my room, and then I'd had to fumble through my shoulder bag to find my key card. She was playing with my breasts from behind me, tweaking and tugging and pinching my nipples until I was ready to scream from ache and desire and need. I had some more vague memories—of kissing passionately once the door slammed shut behind us, tearing at her clothes with the reckless abandon and a heated need that only alcohol and a far-too-long period of celibacy combined could create.

I didn't like to think about how long it had been since I'd been with another woman.

I got her clothes off her and shoved her back against the wall yet again as she smiled at me and tilted my head back, pressing her lips against mine, stoking my inner furnace so hot I finally grabbed her hand and shoved it between my legs. She smiled lazily at me, and somehow we wound up naked in bed, me on top of her, exploring every inch of her body with my hands, my mouth, my tongue. I'd once known that body so well that I could bring her to the edge without even having to think about what I was doing, but this time I wanted to drive her insane with desire, almost punish her for leaving me all those years ago, reminding her of what I did for her, how I'd always satisfied her in ways no other woman could...

Age had taken a toll on both of our bodies since the last time we'd been together—breasts maybe not as firm, hips a bit thicker, skin not as elastic—but her lips had felt good against mine, her skin like silken velvet to my touch, and then she'd flipped me onto my back and reminded me why I'd missed her in my bed.

I slipped out of the bathroom, my coffee in hand. She was still snoring, an arm flung awkwardly over her face. Her hair was also tangled and snarled, her mouth open, and the blanket had crept down a bit, exposing the tops of her breasts. I felt another, treacherous rush of desire and hurried out into the living room before my body betrayed me for a second time in less than twenty-four hours. The living room curtains were open, and the brightness of the day almost blinded me for a moment before I sank down on the couch.

I wanted to jump out the window.

How could you have been so stupid, Tracy?

This was not how I thought running into Dani again would play out whenever I thought about it. I'd imagined it so many times, sitting alone in my house on the sofa with the cats curled up beside me as I drank glass after glass of wine with some horribly saccharine-sweet romantic comedy playing on my big-screen television. I'd imagined throwing a drink in her face and screaming at her, I'd imagined being coldly polite and aloof—pretty much visualized it any number of ways, each more satisfying to me than the last. Some of those scenes had actually made it into my romance novels—but my fictional couples always overcame every obstacle I'd thrown in their path, riding off into the sunset together at the end to live happily ever after. But every single first draft of those novels had an original ending where the injured party refused to forgive her faithless or heartless or insanely stupid love interest, which I of course had to change to get the damned things published. How many murder victims had I based on Dani in the Laura novels, if I were going to be completely honest with myself? More than just one, actually, which is not something of which one should be proud. But I'd never once imagined that when Dani and I finally saw each other again after all those years and all of the heartache and lonely nights, we'd end up in bed together.

Stupid fucking prosecco.

Why had I allowed myself to get so stinking drunk?

Jerry had refilled my glass twice more at the opening reception, and I had no idea what time it was when I saw Dani descending the stairs to the courtyard. I had a pretty healthy buzz going by then and I felt my heart leap when I saw her. When she spotted me, she smiled her most dazzling smile, the one that always made me a little weak and more than a little malleable, and made her way through the chattering crowd in my direction. Jerry saw her coming, so he topped off my glass one last time from the prosecco bottle before vanishing into the crowd, leaving me alone to deal with my ex. She stopped at the bar and got a plastic cup of red wine before joining me where I was standing off to the side, watching the crowd. I knew I needed to get some more food into my stomach, but perversely waited as I sipped from the prosecco.

It was *delicious*. Jerry had excellent taste in liquor.

"There you are," Dani said with her big smile still in place, taking a sip of the wine and wincing.

"The red's undrinkable," I said, trying not to laugh at the expression on her face.

"Yes, I'd noticed," she replied, glancing at my cup. "What're you drinking?"

"Prosecco," I replied with a big grin. "Jerry has a bottle stashed somewhere." I waved my hand. "He keeps filling me up." I frowned at the bubbly liquid.

"You're *drunk*." She laughed, quite pleased, and took another sip from her cup. She shuddered and tossed it into a nearby trash receptacle. "I suppose now's the time to ask you for a favor." She stepped in so close I could smell her perfume. Opium, like always.

"Let me guess—you're covering the murder and you want my story." I really did have the most delightful buzz going. It had lifted my spirits and put me in a really good mood. It's quite marvelous, actually—this is why I love prosecco, and also why it's dangerous for me to drink it. "I suppose I should be offended," I went on, musing out loud. "Is that the real reason you found me and wanted to talk?" I resisted the urge to reach over and pinch her cheek.

Oh, prosecco! You are a harsh mistress.

She sighed. "You always have to make me out to be some kind of monster. And okay, I *was* an absolute shit to you ten years ago, okay? I admit it, are you happy now? If you'd been willing to talk to me then—"

"I'm in a good mood now." I glowered at her. "Don't spoil it for me."

"Can't we let the past be the past and be friends now?" Dani's voice was earnest, and I didn't think it was all an act.

"That *would* be nice," I replied with a smile. I patted her arm with my free hand. "I admit I'm a little oversensitive when it comes to you. But I don't think anyone would blame me for it, do you?"

I'd like to say the prosecco was doing the talking for me, but it wasn't. It did feel good to be talking to her again. And she still was a damned attractive woman. Bygones could be bygones, and caution to the wind, water under the bridge—all of it. Ten years was ten years.

"Of course not." She sighed. "But you're right, I am covering the story and I would like to hear what you have to say—you don't have to go on camera if you don't want to." She glanced around. "You want to get out of here and go somewhere we can talk? Some place where I can get a *decent* glass of red wine?" She glanced over at my cup with a smile. "Or some prosecco?"

"Sure," I remember slurring, and followed her out of the party and down the street. We wound up at the Rib Room at the Royal Orleans Hotel, and she ordered us a bottle of prosecco—which was exactly what I didn't need. It was delicious, and I was more than happy to slurp it down like water as my buzz deepened. She also ordered some appetizers. Once we had our plates of chicken fingers and mozzarella sticks, I told her what I had seen. I could see the disappointment on her face.

"That's it?" she'd said. "You really didn't see anything, then? You wouldn't lie to me, would you?"

"I would be lying if I said anything else. It's all in the police report, which surely you've managed to get a copy of—you're too good at your job not to have, right?" I hiccupped and took another drink. This prosecco wasn't as good as the bottle Jerry had at the party, but it was working just fine for me.

Maybe a bit too well.

"I wish." She shook her head. "I haven't been able to yet, and my sources at the station aren't being helpful at all." Her face darkened. "That prick Randisi hates me." She ran a hand through her hair, which somehow managed to fall back perfectly into place.

"I didn't like him." I frowned and finished my glass, covering my mouth to conceal the burp. "Pompous sexist asshole."

"Yeah, well, a couple of years ago I exposed his partner on the force for taking bribes. He's had it in for me ever since. Like it's my fault his partner was corrupt." She rolled her eyes. "I'm sure he had a rough time with Internal Affairs for a while, but he kept his own nose clean—well, at least they weren't able to hang anything on him. And I didn't find any evidence that Randisi was crooked. But the fucker holds a grudge."

I was really far too drunk at that point to be out in public, let alone drinking more. "Fuck him." I sounded like I was slurring, and the edges of my vision were getting fuzzy.

Dani laughed and refilled my glass. "It's nice to be sitting with you in a bar again, just talking." She took a deep breath. "I am sorry about how everything went down between us."

"You hurt me," I remember replying, admitting something I wouldn't have in a million years had liquor not loosened my tongue. "Really bad, Dani. How could you do that to me? After my parents died and my brother—" I felt my eyes filling up with tears, so I took a deep breath and wiped at them with a cocktail napkin. I was damned if I was going to let Dani see me cry. I hadn't let her when it all went down, and I sure as hell wasn't going to ten years later.

She placed her hand on top of mine. "It was awful of me, I know. But you were shutting me out, Trace. You just kept getting colder and colder. I felt like you didn't want me around anymore." She squeezed my hand. "And I need to feel needed, and you weren't giving me that. I'm sorry."

After that, things were vague. I knew we talked about a lot of things, but I really couldn't remember much of anything else. It was all foggy, other than bringing her back here and letting her spend the night.

And wild, drunken, crazy insane hang-from-the-ceiling sex, of course. I remembered that all too well.

I sighed and took another swig of my coffee. Things were going to be awkward when she woke up. I just hoped she remembered as little of the evening as I did.

I got up and picked up the clothes scattered all over the entryway and living room floors, separating mine from hers. I picked up my pants and the magnifying glass flash drive fell out of my pocket.

Jesus Christ, how could I have forgotten this?

I opened the bedroom door—she was still dead to the world. It really was amazing how deeply she could sleep. I'd always envied that about her, especially on nights when my insomnia was dialed up and I just lay there in bed next to her staring at the ceiling. Alarms didn't work for her—she slept through them. I would hit snooze and try to stay in bed longer, but not Dani. When we'd lived together her damned alarm would have gone on ringing for hours had I not woken up almost immediately and shaken her awake.

I closed the door as softly as possible—just in case—and sat down at the desk. I hesitated for just a moment before plugging the drive into one of my laptop's USB ports. Hopefully, my computer could read it. I could hear the drive whirring as the operating system tried to decipher its contents.

After a few moments, it appeared on my desktop as an external drive named *Demi's Backup*. I let out a sigh of relief and smiled to myself. I clicked on it to bring up the file directory. There were three folders: *WIP, Old Stuff,* and *Images*. I clicked on *Old Stuff,* but there didn't seem to be anything of interest there; all the subfolders were named in a kind of shorthand that made no sense to me, but I could see that everything inside was Word documents. *Surely she wasn't just giving me her goddamned work-in-progress to read?* I thought as I clicked that folder closed. It wouldn't be the first time someone pushed his or her work on me to read and evaluate. I always try to be polite when people ask if I will read their work or if I can recommend them to my agent and/or publisher. It wasn't like I had this overabundance of free time to read the work of a total stranger. I had papers to grade, books of my own to write, and wasn't I entitled to some free time to read for pleasure or watch television or drink wine or—no, I didn't need to justify myself to a stranger. I opened the *WIP* folder—again, a series of Word documents, titled Chapter One through Chapter Thirteen.

I opened the *Images* folder and started clicking through the images, which showed up as thumbnails in the next column of the directory. The first ones were pictures of an airplane and scenes from an airport—obviously, Demi had been documenting every step of her trip. There were several shots of the airplane cabin, mostly the backs of people's heads and their seat backs, but apparently she was trying to get a picture of a male flight attendant. When I got to one of him pushing a cart next to her row, I saw why. He was rather attractive, if you liked men—short dark hair, deep dimples, full lips, his uniform shirt clinging tightly to his muscles. I rolled my eyes and kept scrolling. I recognized the airport in New Orleans, shots from a cab heading east on I-10 coming into the city, the Vieux Carré/French Quarter exit sign, the highway view of St. Louis Cemetery. There were some photos of the entry hallway of the Maison Maintenon, and then some pictures of the pool, taken from her room. The table I'd sat at was clearly visible, and I could also see the door to the room on the second-floor gallery that must have been Antinous's room.

And there was the blurry figure of a man walking down the gallery from the left.

My heart started racing. Had Demi actually photographed the killer?

He was still blurry in the next image, but the third image showed him no longer walking. He had his back to the camera, and I didn't recognize him. I tried to zoom in on him, but the bigger I made his image, the more pixilated it became. Maybe a computer expert could blow it up more clearly than I could— my own computer skills were pretty limited.

In the next picture, the door to the room was open, and he was going inside.

I saw him.

I heard her saying it again, and then the look of horror on her face as she saw something—or someone—over my shoulder.

I cursed myself for being so distracted by Dani's appearance that I hadn't paid attention to her.

"Do you mind if I make a cup of coffee?"

Startled, I jumped and spun around in my chair. Dani had put on one of the guest robes the hotel provided, and belted it tightly. Somehow, she managed to simply look a little disheveled, rather than the mess I always looked when I woke up.

Seriously, a comb through her hair and some makeup and she'd be ready to go on the air. I'd always envied her that.

She crossed the room and kissed my forehead. "What are you looking at?"

Uh-oh, I thought, biting my lower lip. *Not a good sign.* "I'm not really sure," I said slowly, finally deciding *what the hell.* I wasn't an investigator, I wasn't a cop, and she was a reporter. It was her story. "A woman named Demi something gave me this yesterday—you remember her? She interrupted us in the Carousel Bar, said she needed to talk to me? I went outside the bar with her?"

"Yeah, I wasn't sure you were actually going to come back." Dani squinted at the screen. "Is that—is that the room where the victim was staying? She gave you a photograph of the killer going into the victim's room?" She was wide awake now. "Can you tell who it is?"

"No, I can't." I frowned. "There's just blurry images of him from the side and from behind, and I don't pay enough attention to men's asses to tell them apart." I tried to zoom in on the image again, to no avail. "I'm not good enough at this sort of thing to get a decent look at him." I leaned back in the desk chair. "I need to just turn this over to the police and be done with it." The thought of calling Detective Randisi wasn't appealing.

"Well…" She leaned over me and clicked on the directory. Her fingers flew over the keyboard as she copied the *Images* folder onto my desktop. She still smelled slightly of sweat and sex. "There." She stood up when she finished. "Now you can turn the jump drive over to the police for evidence, but you have a copy of the pictures. Can you email them to me? Please? I'd owe you."

"I don't know how I feel about that," I said slowly. "They really aren't mine to do anything with—they belong to Demi. And they're evidence. I wouldn't put it past that Randisi dickhead to charge me with obstruction or something."

"She gave them to you, didn't she?" Dani replied. "She wouldn't have done that if she wanted you to just keep them for her. And even though it's evidence, there's no law that says you can't keep a copy for yourself or share them with your favorite investigative reporter. You do have to turn the pictures over to the cops, but you aren't breaking any laws by copying them."

I wasn't sure I should believe her. "Yeah." I closed my laptop and stood up, stretching. My back cracked in several places, which felt really good.

"You said you wanted coffee?" I asked as I walked past her back into the bedroom. "The coffeemaker's in the bathroom."

"Sure." She followed me into the bedroom, sitting down on the edge of the bed. "I really need to brush my teeth—I don't suppose you have a spare?"

"No, but if you call Housekeeping they'll bring one up." I put a new K-Cup into the coffeemaker and filled it with water. I caught a glimpse of myself in the mirror and sighed, reaching for my brush. My hair looked like a rat's nest, the way it always did when I woke up in the morning. The cottonmouth was pretty much gone, and so was the little headache.

"Shall I order breakfast, too?"

I closed my eyes and sighed to myself. "No, we can go down and have the buffet in the restaurant."

It probably doesn't speak well to my character that what I really wanted was for her to get dressed and leave. I didn't want to pretend or play along, even for another minute, that things were better between us now, or God forbid, that this was the first step in getting back together with her.

Fucking prosecco, anyway.

But it would be nice to be friends with her and not have to worry about running into her whenever I came into town. We had a shared history, and we both had experienced deeply painful losses. As hard as it had been on me when my parents were killed or when I'd watched my brother's slow decline into death, it was just as hard to watch your partner slowly die. I wouldn't wish that on anyone, even though, really, it was something you had to factor in when you were involved with someone.

My, wasn't I wise in the morning after a drunken debauch with an ex? I heard her asking for a toothbrush and splashed some more water on my face once I finished brushing my recalcitrant hair so it looked somewhat presentable.

I started another cup for me once hers was finished, and she took it from me gratefully.

"I forgot how potent prosecco can be," she said, putting the coffee down on the nightstand. "Thanks for letting me stay last night, and…" Her voice trailed off and her face flushed.

Glad I'm not the only one feeling awkward.

I sat down next to her on the bed and took both of her

hands in mine. "Look, Dani—I'm not going to say last night was a mistake"—*even though that is exactly what I think*—"and I am really glad we're now at a place where we can talk and be friends"—*that's sincere, I really do mean that*—"but as far as anything else, I—I don't know."

I was a little taken aback by her obvious relief. "Oh, thank God." She leaned over and kissed me on the cheek, a quick friendly little peck that meant nothing. "I was so worried when I woke up and realized where I was! The last thing in the world I ever want to do is hurt you again, Tracy." She ran a hand through her hair. "It's too soon for me—Mary hasn't even been dead a full year yet. I feel like—I feel like I cheated on her." She bit her lower lip and I was surprised to see tears form in her eyes. "I know that's a shitty thing to say to you, given—well, you know—but I've missed you so much! I don't know."

"Friends is fine with me," I replied, trying to inject some warmth and feeling into my voice, hoping that if I could convince her, I could convince myself as well. "Anything else, well, we'll just have to wait and see."

I was saved by a knock on the door, and Dani bounded out of the bedroom to get her new, hotel-issue toothbrush. I walked back into the bathroom and shut the door, leaning against it and staring at myself in the mirror.

You still have feelings for her, I told my reflection. *Even after all this time, you still have feelings for her.*

Dani returned and knocked on the bathroom door. When she was finished brushing her teeth, she frowned at herself in the mirror. "I should really get my car out of the lot, go home and change clothes." She smiled at me. "It's bad enough having to do the walk of shame this morning, but I don't want people to see me in the restaurant wearing the same clothes!

Tell you what, I'll run home and come back and we can have lunch. Would that be okay? We can talk some more about the case—if that's okay with you?"

I nodded. "I'm going to take the jump drive back to Demi and tell her she needs to turn the photos over to the cops. If she doesn't want to, I'll have to."

"Great." We exchanged numbers, plugging them into our respective cell phones. "I'll text you when I'm almost here, okay?"

Once Dani was gone, I jumped into the shower and got cleaned up as quickly as I could. I couldn't stop thinking while the water coursed over my body, no matter how hard I tried.

The truth was—the guy in those pictures sort of looked like Jerry.

Was that why he'd been late to meet me for dinner on Thursday? Because he was too busy killing Antinous?

I shook my head.

There was simply no way I could ever believe that Jerry was a killer.

And why would he kill Antinous? It didn't make any sense. The proper thing to do, of course, was talk to him—but I did want to talk to Demi first. It was worrisome that I hadn't seen her since she'd given me her flash drive—and that her friends hadn't, either. The fact she wasn't at the party was a bit of a concern as well.

I put on a pair of jeans and a green SLU T-shirt after pulling my hair back into a ponytail. I made sure I had everything I needed and hurried out of the hotel.

It felt like it was going to rain at any moment when I stepped outside. Royal Street was bumper-to-bumper traffic, and in the heavy air the smell of exhaust was horribly nauseating. I hurried down Royal Street and up Toulouse to the Maison Maintenon. The big, heavy front door was open, and I climbed the steps to the entryway. There was someone standing at the registration desk, and I just breezed right past like I had every right to be there. I climbed the hanging, curved staircase in the next room and headed for the outdoor stairs. I walked over to the railing and realized that the angle was wrong from this floor—Demi's room had to be on the third floor. I was sweating as I climbed the stairs to the next level, and sure enough, there was a flash, a crack of thunder, and the temperature dropped at least ten degrees as fat drops of rain started falling from the darkened sky. The wind had definitely picked up, but the building on the other side of the pool courtyard helped block it somewhat. I got a little wet when I went to the railing but was able to confirm that this was the right floor—and the door to my right with 323 on it in gold-painted numbers was undoubtedly Demi's room.

I took a deep breath and knocked—and the door opened a crack.

"Demi?" I called out softly. "It's Tracy Norris. Can I come in and talk to you for a moment?"

Another roar of thunder drowned out any possible response that could have come from inside, so I knocked again, louder. The door swung farther open—

—and I could see a pair of feet sticking out from the other side of the bed.

"Demi? Are you all right?" I called, stepping into the room.

It wasn't until I got to the side of the bed that I could see the staring eyes and the puddle of blood.

CHAPTER EIGHT

I don't know how long I stood there, staring at the body. At least this time I didn't scream.

Goose bumps came up on my arms. The air conditioner kicked on again as I stood there directly underneath the vent, and I rubbed my arms to try to warm up my skin. I knew I was in borderline shock, and probably the best thing to do was go back outside into the heat and humidity. I took some deep breaths and could hear the thudding of my heartbeat in my ears. I managed to somehow reach into my shoulder bag and dig through all the debris and crap with my hand until I found my phone. I'd forgotten to charge it overnight—across the screen were the words *Less than a 20% charge left*—but I managed to touch the keypad icon and dial 911 for the second time in three days.

This is why I don't go to writers' conferences flashed through my mind, and I almost laughed out loud. I realized I was verging on hysterical and willed myself to remain calm while I spoke to the woman who took my call. I robotically answered her questions after telling her that there was a dead body again at the Maison Maintenon.

I can only imagine what the reviews on Yelp were going to say.

She told me an ambulance and the cops were on their way, and I hung up, dropping the phone back into my bag. I was coming back into myself—the initial shock was past, even if I was still freezing; Demi must have turned her goddamned thermostat down to about fifty degrees—and knew I should go back outside to wait for the cops and paramedics—*not that there's anything they can do, she's been dead for quite a while*—and think about the inevitable interview I was going to have with Detective Randisi.

Interrogation, more likely. If you think he was a sexist asshole Thursday night, he's going to be in rare form today. Two corpses, and both times I'm on the scene. Yeah, that's going to go over well.

If this happened in one of my books, of course, my point would be to make the person look really guilty to Laura. But this was real life, not fiction.

Remember how this feels for the next time you have Laura stumble over a body.

But wouldn't that be in incredibly poor taste?

Go outside. Staying in here with a dead body isn't doing your mental state any good.

I closed my eyes, controlled my breathing, and counted to ten.

It worked, as it always did. My heartbeat slowed down to a more normal rate, and I felt more like myself.

I've always been good in a crisis.

And as long as I didn't touch anything or move around, it wouldn't hurt to have a look around, would it?

The air conditioner turned off, and I rubbed my arms again. It was fucking freezing in Demi's room, and I couldn't help but think *that's probably going to wreak havoc with estimating the time of death* as I willed myself to look at the body again.

I couldn't look at Demi yet with her wide, staring eyes, so I looked around the room. The wreckage of a MacBook Pro—the same kind of laptop I used—lay scattered around on the carpet just to the side of the corpse. The power cord was still plugged into a socket to the side of the nightstand—she'd obviously had it set up on the nightstand, which struck me as weird. There was very little room for anything other than the lamp and the telephone, both of which had been shoved to the back to make room for it. I mentally shrugged. I preferred to sit at a desk or a table when I was using mine, but different strokes and all that—everyone has a different method, which is something I emphasized over and over to my writing students. *Find the method that works for you and stick to it.*

Focus, Tracy.

Her MacBook Pro must have been the murder weapon—it looked like the killer had picked it up and clubbed her on the side of the head with it. I could see where it had connected with the side of her face, and she'd gone down on her side. She was wearing the same thing she'd been wearing when she spoke to me outside the Carousel Bar. The killer had apparently just reached for whatever was convenient to use.

So it wasn't premeditated—which was small comfort to Demi.

The killer hadn't come to her room intending to kill her.

So, he or she didn't know about the pictures she had? Of the killer going to Antinous's room?

Her laptop was destroyed, so the originals were gone unless some tech could put the thing back together again.

Maybe the memory chip was intact and could just be put into another one.

But other than the wreckage of the computer and the body on the floor, the room was very tidy. She was obviously very fastidious. The closet door was ajar, and I could see her shoes neatly lined up inside. It looked like she'd hung up her clothes by color, as well. The bed was still made, but given her skin tone and the gelid look of the blood on the side of her face, she had most likely been murdered yesterday during the early evening—probably not long after she'd given me the flash drive and fled from the Monteleone Hotel.

Her friends hadn't seen or heard from her after that, as I recalled them telling me at the reception, and yet—

The door had opened when I'd knocked on it. Had they not stopped by her room to check on her?

That seemed peculiar to me. They were all staying here and had planned on going to the party together. Why wouldn't they have come by and knocked on her door before they headed over to the party? I certainly would have, especially if the friend I had plans with wasn't answering my calls or responding to my texts. And I hadn't knocked very hard on the door. If my light knock got the door to swing open, surely their knock would have as well. So why didn't they come by to check up on her?

Yeah, that was definitely odd. And if not before the party, why wouldn't they have checked on her after?

Focus on the details, Tracy.

I inhaled again. The room smelled musty. The walls were painted a dark emerald green, with gold fleur-de-lis stenciled at regular intervals. The room itself was long and narrow—there was a small kitchenette with a sink, a coffeemaker, and a microwave on the granite counter, with a large white old-model refrigerator shoved into the corner. The bathroom door was closed, and the carpet was dingy looking. It looked brownish now, but had probably been gold to match the fleur-de-lis on the walls at one point. Of course, there was a wide dark stain around her head from the blood.

They're going to have to replace this carpet.

Thick gold-and-green brocade curtains hung on the wall farthest from the front door, which was where undoubtedly she'd stood at the window and taken pictures of the pool courtyard—

Was I in those shots?

I cursed myself for not thinking to look. I'd been so focused on trying to identify the man on the second-floor gallery I hadn't thought to check anything poolside. If I was actually in the pictures, that would give me—well, the police—an idea of the time frame and whether that man was the actual murderer.

Well, at least Dani had been smart enough to copy the images onto my laptop—because I was going to have to turn the flash drive over to the cops now for sure.

If she was killed because of those pictures—

A wave of nausea swept over me, and feeling light-headed, I stepped back outside the door. I started to reach for the doorknob to pull the door closed—but remembered in the nick of time that I shouldn't touch anything. I could hear police sirens getting closer.

No one knows you have the flash drive, so calm down, Tracy. No one besides Dani, that is, and I doubt she's *the killer.*

That made me feel a little better, but I was still nervous. The flash drive was burning a hole in my shoulder bag.

I looked at my watch and was amazed to see I'd only been inside Demi's room maybe five or seven minutes at the most—it seemed like I'd been in there for hours. I swallowed, and shivered. The rain had gotten heavier and was coming down really hard now, big fat drops of water that smacked against the railing of the landing. The wind had also picked up and was driving the heavy drops almost to where I was standing. I took another few steps back as I felt some rain mist on my arms, and the goose bumps came up again. It felt like the temperature had dropped about twenty degrees while I'd been inside, and the blasts of wind were bone-chillingly cold.

The sounds of police sirens got louder and finally stopped entirely just as lightning flashed blindingly close, followed by thunder so loud the building seemed to shake and my teeth went on edge.

A few moments later, the door to Room 322 opened and Pat came out, closing the door behind her and checking to make sure it was locked. She had a black purse over her shoulder and was wearing jean shorts and one of those horrible T-shirts reading *I got Bourbon-faced on shit Street* with the drunk guy with Xs for eyes leaning on a lamp post. She turned and started in surprise when she saw me standing by the stair railing. "Well, hello," she said hesitantly, a confused look on her face. "What are you doing here, Tracy?"

"I came by to talk to Demi," I replied slowly, watching her face for her reaction. *Might as well get it over with.* "I'm afraid I have some bad news for you."

She blinked at me. "Bad news?"

"I'm afraid she's dead, Pat." I said it flatly, without emotion.

She blinked at me a few more times, her forehead crinkled

in confusion. "Dead?" She frowned. "Is that supposed to be some kind of joke? If so, it's not very funny and really in bad taste, given what happened here the other night." Her voice was very much mom-giving-recalcitrant-child-a-lecture. "You really should be ashamed of yourself."

"I wish it were a joke," I replied. I gestured toward the door to Demi's room with my head. "I knocked and her door wasn't closed—I walked in and there she was, on the floor."

All the color drained out of her face, and she leaned heavily against the door to her own room. "Oh my God." She still had her room key in her hand, so she shoved it into the lock and opened the door. She backed into the room, not taking her eyes from my face until I could no longer see her. Worried, I walked over to her door and looked inside. She plunked down on the edge of her bed, looking confused and worried. She looked at me again, unbelieving. "Dead. Demi is dead."

"I'm afraid so, Pat." I took the liberty of walking into her room and sat down next to her on the edge of the bed. I put my arm around her shoulders, and she didn't react to my touch at all. I noticed she was shivering a little bit. Her room was just as cold as Demi's had been.

"I can't believe it," Pat went on in a toneless voice. "How did this happen? Why? Who would want to kill her?" She turned her head to look at me, and her eyes were glassy and watery. "Demi wouldn't hurt anyone, ever."

"I don't know who did it," I replied softly. "It looks like someone picked up her laptop and clubbed her with it."

A hand flew up to her mouth, and tears started coming from her eyes. "Oh, no. Oh, my God." She choked up, and I tightened my grip on her shoulders as she shook with sobs.

"You didn't see or talk to her at all after she left the

Monteleone yesterday afternoon?" I prodded gently. "When she walked out of the bar with me was the last time you saw her?" I didn't add the qualifier *alive*.

She put her head down on my shoulder and wiped at her eyes. "N-no." She took a deep breath. "After she walked out of the bar with you, I never saw her again. Wow—I—I'm never going to see her again!" She broke out into sobs again, and I patted her shoulder helplessly. I am really terrible in these kinds of situations.

She picked her head up again. "Her husband! Her kids! What am I going to tell them?"

Husband and kids?

"Demi was straight?"

"She always told everyone she was bi, but she hadn't been with another woman since college, and that was twenty years ago." Pat nodded. "She was more bi-curious, if anything, really. I mean, I didn't know her when she was in college, but from everything she told me, it was more about where she was at emotionally than actually really being into women, if that makes any sense. She'd been with a real dick of a guy, abusive physically and emotionally, and she was fragile, and this other woman came along and kind of helped her put the pieces back together again...and then she met the guy she eventually married, and that was it for women for her. I think—I think maybe if she hadn't gotten married..." Her voice trailed off. "All of her fiction was from a bi or lesbian perspective. She was actually quite a good writer. I think she was brainwashed into who she was supposed to be, if that makes any sense? The longing in her stories..." She wiped at her eyes. "She was an amazing writer, actually—her short stories would just break your heart. I encouraged her to come to this event...I thought maybe if she got away from her suburban soccer mom existence it might do her some good—and she deserved a break from being wife and mother, you know?" A soft sob escaped from her lips. "Why did I tell her to come? She'd be alive if I hadn't talked her into coming!"

I grabbed her wrists firmly. "Do *not* blame yourself for this, Pat. It isn't anyone's fault except the bastard who killed her."

"But why would anyone kill Demi? She was such a nice person. She'd do anything for anyone without complaint. All you had to do was ask her…all she ever wanted was what was best for people. This was her first trip anywhere without her family. Writing was her dream, the one thing that was really hers, you know?"

"Did you know her family?" I thought it was best to keep her talking. She was on the edge of going into either shock or hysterics or both, and it was the least I could do.

Pat shook her head. "No, I live in Denver. She's from Arizona—Flagstaff." She cleared her throat. "We actually met because we were in an anthology together, *Fire Down Below,* and I really liked her story and asked the editor to put me in touch with her. We kind of hit it off, and I kind of was giving her career advice. She really was an innocent about everything—how publishing works, how good she was as a writer—I mean, her stories were so powerful, so touching… they made you think." She shook her head slightly. "She just happened to see the submissions call for *Fire Down Below* and wrote a story. She had no idea about anything in the business. It was almost cute how naïve she was."

Sounds like the blind leading the blind to me, I thought, but didn't say anything. "So you encouraged her to write?"

She nodded and sniffled again. "Uh-huh."

I heard heavy steps coming up the stairs. I patted her

shoulder again and got up to look outside. Perfect—it was my old buddy Al Randisi. He was holding a dripping umbrella, and his slacks were wet from the knee down. He wasn't wearing a jacket or a tie, just a white dress shirt with the top buttons undone so I could see curly black-and-gray chest hair.

"You got here pretty fast." I said. Behind him I could see the EMTs coming up the stairs, and some uniformed cops.

"When I heard there was another body here on the radio, I made a beeline over here." He scowled at me. "I might have known you'd be here."

Irritated, I drew myself up to my full height and scowled back at him. "I'm just as delighted to see you again as you are to see me, Detective." I refrained from adding *douchebag*.

He gave me a look as he pulled out a notebook from a shirt pocket and flipped it open. "Tracy Norris, mystery writer." He started writing. "You know, the way you keep popping up at my crime scenes is starting to look kind of funny—what are the odds that the same person would be at two different crime scenes on two different days?" His beady little eyes darted over at me, looking me up and down in a sleazy way that made me feel more than just a little bit dirty. "So, where's today's body?"

I gestured over to the door for Room 323. "In there. The door's not shut—you can just push on it and it'll open." I held up my hands and he gave me an inquiring look. "I didn't touch the knob, and I didn't touch anything inside that I can remember. I knocked and the door opened. I saw her feet and went inside. She's dead, Detective—it's pretty apparent."

He nodded and pushed on the door, going inside when it swung open. I leaned against the wall, feeling weary suddenly. The adrenaline was wearing off and I was starting to feel the shock. I put my hands on my knees and bent over, putting my head down and taking long, deep breaths until my head cleared again. I got out of the way as EMTs carrying equipment walked past me, followed by the uniformed officers.

A few moments later, Randisi came back out. He gestured for me to follow him and led me down the stairs and down a hallway to an enormous sitting room. There was a coffee machine sitting on a bar next to a wicker basket full of muffins and bagels in cellophane. "Have a seat," he said over his shoulder to me. "Want some coffee?"

"Yes, that would be nice." The room was as frigidly cold as every other room in the hotel, and I shivered as I sat down in a red velvet wingback chair that groaned a bit. "Cream and sweetener, if you don't mind."

He sat down in the matching chair on the opposite side of a small table. He set my coffee down on the table and took a drink from his.

"Thanks," I said, picking up the little Styrofoam cup. Granules of the sweetener were floating on top of the liquid. I sighed to myself and took a drink. It was actually better than I would have thought, and I took another sip.

"So," he said, giving me a wry look, "two bodies in three days. That's a record, I think, for an innocent bystander."

"Yeah, well." The coffee was starting to warm me up, which felt good. I leaned back into the chair, holding on to the cup that was now warming my hands. The room was musty-smelling, like every old house in New Orleans. There was a worn carpet on the floor, and large oil paintings hung on the walls. The room was clearly an interior one, since there were no windows. "Believe me, it wasn't by choice. Obviously."

"But this time you knew the victim?"

I nodded. "Only slightly. I don't even know her last name. I just met her for the first time yesterday. She was in my workshop yesterday afternoon." I stifled a laugh.

He gave me a sharp look. "You think it's funny?"

I rolled my eyes. "Of course not, Detective Randisi. It's just that this is almost exactly the same conversation we had Thursday afternoon. I didn't know her well. Her name was Demi something or another. I met her for the first time yesterday morning in the CC's on Decatur. She and some friends are here for the same conference I'm here for. They sat at the next table, and I heard them talking about Antinous Renault's death, and so I talked to them about it. They knew Antinous much better than I did, obviously—I'd never even heard of her before meeting her on Thursday." I quickly went over some of the things we talked about in the coffee shop yesterday morning.

"Sounds like a lot of people at this conference wanted to see Antinous Renault dead." He gave me another look. "Her real name, by the way, was Diana Browning. It was on her passport."

I nodded. "Like I told you Thursday, she never told me her real name, but she did tell me Antinous Renault was a pseudonym. She was apparently a pretty toxic person." I didn't tell him about her blog or her website; I'm sure others he'd talked to already had. It's been my experience the police— no matter how incompetent or stupid—do not appreciate lay people telling them how to do their jobs.

And Detective Randisi definitely wouldn't appreciate any suggestions from me.

On the plus side, he didn't seem as dick-holish this morning as he had on Thursday.

"So, you barely knew this woman yet you came over

here this morning to her hotel room? Why?" He raised his eyebrows.

I reached into my bag. I dug around inside until I found the flash drive and handed it over to him. "I was returning this, and I also wanted to ask her why she'd given it to me in the first place." He listened without reaction as I explained how she'd approached me in the Carousel Bar yesterday and given it to me.

"You think she saw someone that spooked her, and she got out of there?" He kept making notes.

"Yeah. I don't know who or what it was." I spread my hands helplessly. "I wish I knew more."

"And what's on this flash thingy she wanted you to see so badly?"

"There's a folder of pictures," I said carefully. "I looked at them this morning on my computer. She was taking pictures of her arrival—the airport, the cab into the city, the hotel. She took pictures of the pool from her window, and apparently she got some pictures of a man going into Anti—into Diana Browning's room." Calling her *Diana Browning* made it seem less real to me; she'd never been that name, that identity, when she'd been alive to me, so using that name made it seem like the murder had happened to someone else.

"Do you know who the man was? Did you recognize him?"

I bit my lower lip. "He looked familiar, but no, I couldn't say positively I could identify him. I don't make a habit of noticing men, Detective." *Make what you will of that—but if you've investigated the conference you already know I'm a lesbian.* "It was also kind of blurry, and you can't get a really good look at his face or even his head—the angle she was taking the pictures at weren't the best. I mean, he could be anyone, really." I added quickly, "I tried to make the pictures bigger in my computer, to see if I could get a better idea of who it was, but they just pixilated." I held up my hands apologetically. "Sorry."

He made a face. "Too much to hope for, I suppose." He gave me a lopsided smile. "We got some computer people who might be able to do something with it, you never know." He scratched his head. "You been pretty helpful today, Miz Norris."

I couldn't help but raise an eyebrow. He was like a completely different person from the misogynist ass I'd had to deal with Thursday afternoon. Surely he hadn't had a personality transplant since then? "Thank you," I replied cautiously.

"You sure you didn't see or hear anything suspicious?"

"Pretty sure." I closed my eyes and replayed my trip up the indoor hanging staircase, walking along the inside hallway to the open door to the outdoor stairs and hallways. I'd been aware of the coming storm, the coldness of the wind, and trying to stay dry once the rain started. There hadn't been anyone around that I'd seen after I passed the receptionist in the entry hallway. Had I heard someone—something—before I knocked on Demi's door? I honestly couldn't say. "I don't remember, Detective. I'm sorry, but I don't think so."

He pulled out a business card from his shirt pocket and passed it to me. "I know I gave you one of these the other day, but in case you lost it, here's another one. If you think of anything else…" He started to rise as I took the card from him, but then sat back down. "Can you think of any reason why this Demi woman would give you the flash drive?"

"No. It doesn't make any sense to me." I gave a half laugh. "I've been trying to figure it out myself ever since I saw the pictures on there. To be honest, when she gave it to me, I wasn't really paying any attention to her—my mind was somewhere else." I felt my face starting to flush. "A personal issue had come up that I was dealing with—when she asked to speak to me, I was glad for the excuse to get away from the problem and think? She was just my escape…I wish I'd been paying more attention. And once she gave me the envelope and left the hotel, I put it in my pocket and forgot about it as I went back to dealing with the problem." I took a deep breath. He was looking at me inquisitively. "I ran into an ex in the bar, Detective, and it was a pretty bad breakup."

He nodded sympathetically. "That makes sense." He scratched his head. "But you can see my problem here, right?" His voice was soothing, well modulated, almost like he wanted my sympathy. "Why would she give this evidence to you, someone who's practically a stranger?"

I shrugged. "I'm a mystery novelist. Maybe she thought, I don't know, that I was working on the case or something? That I had some kind of police connection? I don't know why people do things, Detective." I held up my hands. "Believe me, I wish I had a better explanation for you."

"You have to admit it, it looks a little weird." He smiled softly, his eyes wide open. "I mean, the woman was killed by her laptop—that's how it looks anyway, and you have this flash drive of information she had on her computer…"

"Surely," I said slowly, trying very hard to keep my temper in check, "you aren't implying that I came by, killed her with her computer, and stole her flash drive? Only to come by this morning to discover her body and turn the flash drive over to the police? That doesn't make sense, Detective."

"Oh, I don't know." He smiled at me, but his dark eyes glittered coldly. "Like you said, you write mysteries. You study crime, you study police procedure to make your books look more real, don't you?" He gave a little shrug. "Maybe you figured it would look better if you were the one to come back and find the body, and happened to turn over the flash drive after deleting whatever it was that was incriminating on it? That would be pretty smart, don't you think?"

I started to fire off a smart-ass answer, but stopped myself. That was probably what he was hoping for. I tapped my fingers on the armrests of the chair. After a few moments of silence, I replied sarcastically, "That might work as the plot of a book, Detective—do you mind if I make a note of that? I'll be sure to thank you in the acknowledgments." I pulled out my phone and typed myself a note, slowly and deliberately. When I finished, I dropped it back into my purse. "As for reality, Detective, I am pretty smart. I do have two doctorates, after all. But I'm not a murderer, and I'd like to think if I was, I'd be even smarter than that." I gave him a very cold smile, knowing I shouldn't say it but did anyway. "I'd like to think if I killed someone I'd be smart enough to never be caught."

To my surprise, he laughed and stood up. "Yeah, didn't think so—but it didn't hurt to put it out there." He stretched, and I heard his back crack. "Don't lose my card, and be sure to call me if you remember anything." He paused at the door. "I downloaded one of your books Thursday night and started reading it. You're pretty good, you know."

The door shut behind him.

CHAPTER NINE

I sat there for a little while in the dimly lit room, a little
shocked. Detective Randisi had actually seemed almost
human. My phone beeped in my bag, and I grabbed it. There
was a text message from Dani: *On my way down.*

I replied, *Pick me up at Maison Maintenon.*

After she replied, I got out of my chair and got another
cup of coffee, musing as I walked out of the room and toward
the hotel's front door. It was still raining, so I stood in the open
doorway, waiting for Dani.

That's when it hit me—*How did the killer know Demi had
the pictures?*

She had to have told the killer—which meant she *knew*
the killer, whoever it was.

She'd recognized him from the blurry pictures, and she
must have confronted him about it after giving me the flash
drive. I thought back to the conversation we'd had, sitting on
that sofa in the lobby of the hotel. No, she hadn't said anything
that I could recall that would be of use to the police. I shivered,

standing there in the doorway. I considered going back upstairs and talking to Pat more, asking her some more questions about Demi and who else at Angels and Demons she might have known. I tried to remember what the two men in their group looked like, tried to compare my memories of them with my memories of the pictures, but it was useless. I hadn't been lying when I said I really didn't notice men all that much. I noticed their faces, but their bodies not so much. The only way I'd recognize the man in the pictures in real life was if he was in front of me and the pictures were, too.

This is why I am not a police detective. I prefer my crimes to be fictional.

It's much more fun when you know already who the killer is from the very beginning.

Cars were crawling by on the street, which was filling slowly with water. There was more lightning and thunder, and it was getting darker out. A cab pulled up in front of the door, and I stood aside so the passengers could dash by, hauling their luggage behind them. *Come on, Dani,* I thought impatiently, resisting the temptation to start tapping my foot. I glanced at my watch as my stomach growled. *That's not going to make her get here any faster.*

To pass the time, I decided to make the case an intellectual challenge for myself: *If I were writing this book, who would I have made the killer?*

I always started with the crime when I was writing, so when I started outlining and planning the book, that was my foundation: *X killed Y, this is why, so who else wanted to kill Y? How did X do it?*

Well, for one thing, I could never get away with having someone kill Antinous—*Diana*—over her online antics and churlish online trolling. The only way that could be a valid motive for murder in a book would be if the killer was mentally unbalanced—which was unfair and a cheat to the readers—or if it was done in the heat of the moment, and a killing over online trolling could *never* be a crime of passion. That was the beauty of being an online troll: You could be as hateful, venomous, and monstrous as you could find it in your shriveled little soul and pay no consequences. Even if your anonymity was blown, no one would ever take the time to track you down and kill you—the target of your venom would forget your horrific behavior almost as soon as they turned off their computer. And even if you made it your stock in trade, as Diana/Antinous seemed to have done with her "review" website, surely no one would stockpile grudges over a period of time and leap at the opportunity to get even?

Especially over book reviews. There was a reviewer in San Francisco who despised every single Laura Lassiter novel I'd published. The first time I'd really been hurt and upset—it was my first book, I was so proud and happy to have gotten an agent and have a book published, the initial reviews from industry journals and major reviewers had been so generous and kind that this nasty review was like getting a two-by-four in the forehead. After I read the clipping, I wondered why my editor had bothered to send it to me. The reviewer, a woman named Andrea Shapiro, spent about seven hundred and fifty words shredding my book, and me personally. The nicest thing she said in the review was *a very third-rate rip-off of Sue Grafton.*

As I stared at the nastiness, I noticed that my editor had included a sticky note in the envelope that had fallen off the review. I picked it up and started laughing.

This one fairly reeks with the stench of failed author, doesn't it?

Andrea Shapiro's nasty reviews became something of a running gag between me and my editor over the years, even though we had both moved on to different publishers and hadn't worked together on a book in years. Every once in a while she'd give me a call and we'd laugh about Andrea Shapiro, who never gave out a good review when she could write a nasty one. I'd been tempted, after one particular hatchet job, to send her some roses with a card reading, *Thanks for the review, third-rate Dorothy Parker!*

So, no, it was hard to believe anyone would have hunted down Antinous/Diana specifically to kill her for her online conduct. Sure, when someone trashed one of your books—and you—unfairly online, you wanted to kill them in that moment. God knows I have. I have wanted to hunt down some assholish reviewers, disembowel them, and set what was left on fire as a public service. But to actually do it? I found it really hard to believe. Even the nonsense she'd spewed about poor Anne Howard wasn't really enough to drive someone to commit murder.

And now the killer—whoever it was—had killed *twice*.

Of course, I was assuming that the two crimes were related—but what were the odds that they weren't? Pretty long, I would think. Neither crime had been a robbery—surely Randisi would have mentioned it had someone robbed Diana's room, and as far as I could tell the only thing out of place in Demi's had been the body and the destroyed laptop. The killer, whoever it was, had taken care of Antinous/Diana and thought he'd gotten away with it. No witnesses, no evidence, nothing—only to find out that Demi had unknowingly taken pictures of him outside Antinous/Diana's room. Once the killer knew that, Demi was doomed. The killer had disposed of her at the first opportunity, and again seemed to have gotten away with it. Maybe someone in the hotel had seen something or someone suspicious, but for now, the killer had to be breathing a sigh of relief.

Until, of course, the killer found out about the flash drive.

Then it hit me.

There had been no sign of forced entry into her room—just like with Diana. So, both Diana and Demi had not only *known* their killer well enough to open their doors to him, but felt safe enough with him *to let him into their rooms.*

Neither one of them had recognized that they were opening their doors to death.

Surely there weren't that many men at Angels and Demons that both women knew that well? Diana/Antinous was from England—whom could she possibly have known in the States?

That was the key, I was sure of it.

The more I thought about Demi's behavior in the hotel lobby, the more I remembered she seemed agitated and nervous—but more *surprised* than scared when she saw whoever it was that had so unnerved her she'd run out. Maybe she'd run out after whomever it was she'd seen.

Maybe she had walked back to her hotel with her killer.

You don't know she wasn't scared—are you rewriting and revising your memories to fit a new theory? At the time you thought she was afraid, that was your initial reaction. You didn't really know her at all. Your first instinct was probably the right one. You read her as scared, and why would she have chased after someone she was afraid of?

But if she was afraid, why did she run out of the hotel?

My head was starting to hurt again.

This is why I do not try to solve crimes I am not completely in control over—best to just leave this all to the police.

Besides, I reasoned as lightning struck nearby and thunder set off car alarms, *you're not getting paid to solve this. Leave it to the pros and finish writing your own damned book.*

The rain was still pouring down, and there was now about three inches of water in the middle of the street. The gutters were full of water and the curbs were submerged. The lower parts of the city were probably flooding. Some drenched tourists ran by, holding soaked newspapers over their heads in a vain attempt to keep their heads dry. A blast of wind drove some rain at me, and I backed through the doorway onto the black-and-white parquet floor of the main hallway of the Maison Maintenon. I sighed, annoyed that I hadn't thought to buy an umbrella on the way over here. It had been overcast, and as a New Orleans native I should have known that meant it was going to rain. I was going to get soaked running the short distance from the door to Dani's car when she got here, and my teeth were already starting to chatter.

But at least she *was* coming to get me—otherwise my only option would have been to wait out the rain before heading back to the Monteleone, or get drenched running back over there and risk catching a cold in the arctic climate inside the hotel. My stomach growled, and I remembered I hadn't had any breakfast. It was now past noon. My next panel wasn't until three, so there was plenty of time for me to eat something at the Monteleone restaurant.

A young man came running down the sidewalk toward me. He was holding a newspaper over his head, but his white T-shirt was soaked through and was clinging to his skin like clear wrap, and his khaki knee-length shorts clung to his legs.

His black Keds splashed through the water on the sidewalk as he reached the bottom of the steps below me. He looked vaguely familiar, but I couldn't quite place where I knew him from. He tossed the newspaper aside once he was in the shelter provided by the entryway, and he stood there for a moment, wringing out the bottom of his T-shirt. He smiled at me before turning away and once I got a look at his profile, I knew where I'd seen him before.

He was the guy in the book room who was turning Antinous's books around, the kid that Ted chased away.

"Hello there," I said pleasantly. "Didn't I see you yesterday at the Monteleone, in the book room?"

Startled, he turned and looked at me. "Hello," he muttered. Even though he was on the bottom step, our eyes were almost level, which meant he was a lot taller than I had originally thought. He let go of his wet shirt, which slapped against his stomach. He hadn't shaved and there was stubble scattered over his cheeks, chin, and neck. Water was running down his face from his hairline. He had a slight underbite, so his lower lip was larger and stuck out a bit. He didn't smile back at me. "Maybe. I don't remember."

"Yes, I know I did," I held out my hand, smiling. "I'm Tracy Norris."

He looked at my hand for a moment before taking it. His hand was rough and enormous, swallowing mine. "Kenny Simon."

I kept staring at him. Yes, I'd seen him in the book room, but that wasn't it. He looked so familiar...I knew I'd seen that face before, somewhere else. "Sorry I'm staring, but I'd swear I know you from somewhere besides the book room. Your face is so familiar..."

The scowl disappeared, replaced by a smile that lit up his

entire face. "Well, I model," he said, shyly looking down at his feet and shifting his weight from one leg to the other. "I've been on a couple of book covers, and I've done some print work." His face began to slowly turn red.

And in that moment, I saw it. I knew exactly where I'd seen him before. Rather than the short dark hair, I pictured his oval face and pronounced cheekbones surrounded by long sausage curls and a silk shirt with billowing sleeves, opened to expose a smooth chest with enormous nipples.

"You're on the book cover for *The King's Sword*," I said slowly.

His smile faded immediately and was replaced by a scowl. "Yes," he said abruptly. "I posed for that cover."

"Why were you turning Antinous Renault's books around in the book room the other day?" *In for a penny, in for a pound,* I thought. "So you couldn't be seen on the cover?"

His face flushed, and he chewed on his lower lip for a moment before saying, "It's complicated."

There was no sign of Dani or her car yet, so I smiled and said, in my most sympathetic voice—the one I used to get students to open up to me, "You want to talk about it?" I gestured out at the pouring rain. "I'm not going anywhere, and it might make you feel better if you get some of it out."

"It's embarrassing—really embarrassing. I mean, I…" He flushed even darker and swallowed, his Adam's apple bobbing in his long neck. "I'm so stupid."

"Don't say that. You're not stupid."

"That's because you don't know how stupid I really am." He rubbed his eyes and sighed. "I mean, I really—I really thought the author photo was, you know, her. Him. Whatever. You know what I mean." He swallowed. "You know she pretended to be a man, right? Well, I was stupid enough to believe her."

"A lot of people did," I replied, making my voice soothing, like he was one of my students sitting in my office having a meltdown. "That's nothing to be ashamed of. She and her publisher did a really good job fooling people. Why wouldn't you believe them? I mean, seriously, Kenny. Who would do such a thing? I use a pseudonym, but I don't pretend I'm another person. I use my own face in my jacket photos."

"Yes, well, she sure fooled me, the fucking bitch." He made a sour face and slammed a fist into the palm of his other hand. "I didn't know. I didn't have any idea." He sighed. "I found one of her books at a gay bookstore back home in Atlanta. *The Minstrel's Song.* Have you read it?" His eyes got a little dreamy. "It's about Richard the Lionheart and Blondel the musician. Do you know the story?"

I didn't know the story as told by Antinous/Diana in what I was relatively certain she would have referred to as one of her "meticulously researched" novels, but I knew the history. Norah Lofts had even written a novel about it back in the 1970s called *The Lute Player.* Returning home from the Crusades, Richard the Lionheart was taken prisoner and held captive by Duke Leopold of Austria for several years. Blondel, his favorite minstrel, wandered throughout the Holy Roman Empire, playing songs Richard himself had written, trying to find his missing king. He eventually did, and soon effected Richard's release and return to England. There was a school of thought amongst some modern historians that the Lionheart had actually been gay; his lack of mistresses and disinterest in his wife certainly spoke to a lack of interest in women, at any rate. It wasn't hard to imagine what Antinous's—*Diana's*—

take on the story had been; Lofts herself had made no secret of her belief that the Lionheart was gay. "I'm familiar with the story. In Antinous's novel, I assume King Richard and Blondel were lovers?"

He nodded. "Such a beautiful story, the way she told it, and so romantic. They grew up together as boys and were always together—in her book they fell in love when they first reached manhood. If you know the story you know Richard was a second son, so they didn't really think he'd ever inherit anything other than his mother's duchy of Aquitaine…" He continued on, obviously taking his knowledge of the history of twelfth-century England and France from what he'd read in her "meticulously researched" novel.

A lot of it was, of course, completely wrong.

I would hardly call myself an expert on the period—my PhD in history was focused primarily on a later period in English history—but Richard's mother Eleanor of Aquitaine was one of my favorite females in European history. What feminist wouldn't be fascinated by the true story of the wealthiest and most beautiful heiress in Europe, who wrote poetry and songs and spoke multiple languages? A woman who married a king of France and led a regiment of women on Crusade, who was a patron of poets and musicians, survived a divorce and then married a man eleven years younger who became one of England's greatest medieval kings? She'd been queen of France *and* queen of England. Eleanor of Aquitaine kicked ass, and she lived to be over eighty years old in a time when most women died in childbirth before they were thirty. If I were ever to write historical fiction, I'd write about her.

She was *amazing.*

"It's always nice when you find a novel you can connect with," was all I said when he paused to catch his breath. His enthusiasm for reading was encouraging—if his taste in fiction left something to be desired.

He nodded at me. "I *know*! I love to read, I always have, my parents were always telling me to go outside and play, but I always wanted to just curl up somewhere with a good book. *The Minstrel's Song* just spoke to me in a way no other book I'd ever read before had. I tried to find out everything I could about Antinous Renault online—the way he wrote, and he was just so unbelievably handsome...and that body..." He swallowed. "You know she posted tons of pictures of the model on her website and Facebook page and her blog, right? Shirtless or in Speedos...he was so beautiful—or so I thought. The happiest day of my life was when I tracked down an email address for him so I could send him a fan letter, let him know how much I loved the book. I emailed him." His face darkened. "He answered, very friendly and nice and kind. We started corresponding, through emails and on Facebook and Twitter. He was so nice, and so friendly, and I thought he was interested in me..." He wiped at his eyes. "I sent him pictures. I mean, what did I know? I was just a stupid kid."

"How old were you?"

"I was seventeen when I first got in touch with him. I'm twenty now."

"I see." Inside, I was shaking with rage. Antinous Renault was a worthless piece of *shit*. I could certainly understand being nice to someone emailing you about your book—but Kenny was just a *kid*. And she'd fucked with his mind and emotions, just for the fun of it. I'm sure she justified it to herself in some way—I heard her voice echoing in my head, about how supportive she was of—what was it she called it? Oh yes, "the *Cause*." I'm sure she told herself she was encouraging a gay teen to be true to himself.

If she weren't already dead I would have gladly slapped the shit out of her.

"And you know, he was the one who got me into modeling. He saw some of my pictures on my Facebook page and suggested me to Kyle Bennett to pose for the cover of *The King's Sword*." He tilted his head back. "How could I have been so stupid?"

"She was a con artist," I heard myself saying. "It happens, Kenny."

His face twisted. "And Kyle Bennett is a *perv*."

"Was that your first modeling gig?" I asked softly. "Why do you call him that?"

He nodded. "I spent most of the time fighting him off." He shuddered. "Nasty little troll! Like I would ever sleep with him." He sneered. "That was what he wanted, you know. He kept touching me during the photo shoot—my chest, my butt, my stomach—would brush up against me. Ugh." He shuddered.

"Have you modeled since then?"

He preened. "The photo shoot I did for the book got me a contract with an agency in New York. That's where I live now."

I could see it, actually. He was tall and very lean, broad-shouldered but narrow-hipped at the same time. The strong, square jaw, the underbite with the protruding lower lip, the deep-set green eyes, and the olive skin tone—yes, I could see him on a runway or in a magazine ad. "But that's wonderful! And really, it's because she encouraged you."

His face clouded again. "I thought I was in love with him." He kept saying *him* and using male pronouns, like he refused to accept the reality that Antinous was—had been—a woman. "I was horrified when I found out it was that nasty fat English bitch pretending to be a man the whole time. And she told me I was stupid, you know? She laughed at me." He scowled. "When I found out she was coming here, I decided to come here, too, and show her Kenny Simon isn't anyone to be laughed at or made fun of." His hands clenched into fists. "But someone killed her before I had a chance to confront her about her lies, and the way she just toyed with me." He slammed one of his fists into the palm of his other hand, and I reflexively took a step back. His hands were quite large.

"But you wouldn't have hurt her?"

He shrugged. "I don't know what I would have done to her, honestly. She deserved a lot worse than what she got." He leaned in close to me. "I hope she *suffered*."

I was really glad to see Dani pull up to the curb, and excused myself, running down the steps and dashing for the car. Dani leaned over and opened the door so I could jump right in, pulling the door shut behind me. Through the rain I could see Kenny go inside the hotel. Dani's car had the air-conditioning on full blast, and my teeth started chattering. I'd gotten drenched in the dash to the car, and before she pulled away from the curb she reached into the backseat and handed me a towel. I gratefully dried off my arms and rubbed at my wet hair. "Who was that you were talking to?" she asked as she stopped at the Bourbon Street corner.

I started filling her in on everything that happened since she'd left me to go change her clothes as she drove us down to Decatur Street, then back up Bienville to the Monteleone garage. She pulled in and gave the keys to the valet; I gave my room number and we headed into the icy hotel air-conditioning. "Let's have lunch," I said when we reached the lobby. "I'm starving."

The restaurant wasn't full, and we were seated in a booth

almost immediately. Still shivering, I ordered a cup of coffee to start, and when the waitress brought it, held it in my still-cold hands, hoping its warmth would seep into my skin.

"You might want to change out of those wet clothes," Dani said, glancing at me over the top of her menu. "It's freezing in here, and you're going to catch a cold at the very least."

I took a long drink of the coffee and almost moaned as its blessed warmth worked its way through my body. "I'll be fine, really."

"Are you sure?" Dani put the menu down. "You look a little green around the gills." She rolled her eyes. "My God, I sound like my mother. But seriously, Trace, you found a body this morning and you've been out in the rain. Are you sure you're okay?"

"Surprisingly enough, yes, I actually am." It was true—and now with the coffee working its magic and warming me up, I felt much better. The food would be the final trick—my stomach growled again so loudly Dani's eyebrows went up. "Just hungry." I gave her a sheepish grin.

The waitress returned, took our orders, and disappeared with our menus.

"So, do you think that model could be the killer?" Dani asked once we were alone again.

"I don't know." I frowned and drank some more coffee. "It seems like a big reach—killing someone because they pretended to be someone else?" I made a face. "I mean, I don't even know if I can fault Diana for it, you know? If she was using a male name and had hired someone to pose for author photos—if she was using a male persona, she couldn't very well tell Kenny when he emailed her that she was really a woman. And really, is that enough motivation to kill someone?"

"It motivated him enough to spend the money to come

to New Orleans to confront her," Dani pointed out. "Your problem is that in a book, it has to make sense. In real life, it doesn't have to. People act crazy all the time, do crazy shit. Trust me, I report these kinds of stories all the time and most of the time I just wonder, *how can people act like this?*"

"That's kind of what Detective Randisi said to me." I paused as our waitress placed a glass of iced tea in front of Dani and refilled my coffee. She placed a black plastic carafe next to the little caddy holding the sweeteners, smiled and disappeared yet again. "I mean, I get it—real life isn't nice and neat, and things don't get all wrapped up in a nice package with a bow on it at the end. But I can't believe he came all the way here to kill her. I can't believe someone would actually fall in love with someone they've never met in person."

"You really need to start watching more television," Dani replied with a grin. "MTV even has a reality show about this sort of thing. It's called 'catfishing.' It happens a hell of a lot more than you think it does."

"Catfishing?"

Dani nodded. "These people go online and invent a whole new identity, use other people's pictures, and start having relationships with people online that are all based on this lie. And sometimes it goes on for years…seriously. Don't make that face at me." She pulled out her phone and played with it, finally turning it and showing me the screen. "See?"

I stared at the screen. She'd pulled up a website that was all about the catfishing phenomenon. I read it, not quite believing what I was reading.

People actually sent money to people they'd never actually met in person. They became engaged to them.

I handed her the phone back. "People never cease to amaze me."

"So, you see?" She put her phone back into her bag. "He could have really thought he was in love with her as a man." She crossed her eyes. "And had his heart broken when he found out she'd been playing him for a fool. It's not a far leap to go from love to hate, you know. Those feelings have to go somewhere."

"I don't know what to think, to be honest." I stared into my coffee cup. "On the one hand, I feel sorry for her. I mean, I chose to be Winter Lovelace, but I've also never hidden that I'm also Tracy Norris. Different genres, but there's plenty of crossover. And it's not like I hired someone to pretend to be Winter, you know? It just seems weird that a publisher would force her to do that."

Publisher.

Kyle Bennett.

What was it Kenny had said about him?

Like I would ever sleep with him. That was what he wanted, you know. He kept touching me during the photo shoot—my chest, my butt, my stomach—would brush up against me.

"I wonder if her being exposed hurt her publisher?" I gnawed on my lower lip. "But he had to know she was a woman, not a man."

Dani rolled her eyes. "If he was smart, he'd deny any knowledge of the deception—that's how I'd play it. If she was completely vested in her masquerade and he never actually met her or spoke to her in person or on the phone, he might have thought she was a man, too."

"Well, he's actually here this weekend." I made a face. "His name is Kyle Bennett—I met him the night of the murder. He wanted Jerry to have some kind of memorial thing for her at the opening reception. Jerry basically told him to fuck off."

"Do you know who the guy is that pretended to be Antinous Renault?" Dani asked. "That's who I'd like to speak to." She grinned at me. "He could probably fill in all kinds of blanks."

"Well," I said with a startled shake of my head, "there he is, in the flesh. And he's with Kyle Bennett and Jerry."

Chapter Ten

Dani didn't even attempt to be nonchalant—she was never good at it, anyway. I actually could remember a time when I found her lack of subtlety to be almost charming at best and a bizarre personality quirk at worst. I'd often wondered how she managed to do her job so well—and likewise, how she managed to keep her job given her almost utter lack of anything remotely resembling tact.

I sighed audibly as she didn't even try to hide what she was doing. She turned around in her chair and stared so obviously that some people at nearby tables also glanced in that direction, but with a little more decorum.

The three men were standing in front of the hostess's desk as she talked on the telephone while messing around at her computer. Kyle Bennett was in the middle, and I couldn't help but notice that Jerry and the Model Formerly Known as Antinous Renault were standing almost too close to him—so close they looked sort of like a police escort, hemming him in so he couldn't escape if he tried.

Kyle wasn't a good-looking man under the best of circumstances, but standing between two taller, better-built, and much more handsome men didn't help him at all. He was slouching, the way he always seemed to, and was wearing an extremely unflattering plaid-patterned shirt in varying shades of mustard yellow and green. He was clearly miserable and wanted to be anywhere else but here. I felt rather sorry for him.

I was about to chastise Dani for being so obvious when she stood up and waved, calling Jerry's name. Mortified, I gasped in a loud whisper, "Dani, will you sit *down*?"

Jerry looked in our direction, and a dark scowl spread over his face. The scowl turned to shock when he realized I was sitting at the same table. He said something out of the side of his mouth to his companions before walking around the hostess table and crossing the room with long strides. He was wearing his usual short-sleeved black knit shirt and jeans, with a gold-and-silver cross hanging around his neck on a gold chain. A silver dagger hung from his pierced right ear. His face was flushing red, and there were dark circles under his tan. His eyes were also bloodshot, and ignoring Dani completely, he sat down and asked me, through clenched teeth, "What in the name of all that's holy is Lois Lane doing here?" His voice was even, but he was gripping the arms of his chair with such intensity his knuckles turned white.

Dani slid back down into her chair with a satisfied smile on her face. "Relax, Muscles," she said, using her old nickname for him—one he'd always hated. "Tracy and I—we're all good now, so you don't have to keep being nasty to me for her sake, okay?"

"Maybe you two are," Jerry shot back, not looking at her

but fixing me with an unreadable stare, "but that doesn't mean you and I are, Lois."

I'd forgotten he'd always mockingly called her *Lois Lane.* Jerry had never really liked Dani, never thought she was good enough for me—but was gracious enough to never say "I told you so" when I'd left her. One of his best qualities was his intense loyalty, but he sometimes took it too far. Jerry never forgave people who hurt the people he cared about, and Dani had really hurt me. He'd never forgive her for that, he'd never forget it, and the best thing for me to do right now was divert his attention from her before things got ugly.

"We'll talk later, Jerry." I interrupted them before Dani got a chance to say anything. The last thing I wanted was a scene in the restaurant, and I wanted to know why he was having lunch with the Model and Kyle Bennett. He'd made it pretty clear to me the other night at Muriel's that he despised Kyle, so I wanted to hear the story. With Jerry, there *always* was one. "Lunching with Kyle Bennett *and* the faux Antinous Renault? What is he even doing here? What are you up to?"

Jerry looked back over to his companions, still standing at the hostess stand. The hostess was still on the phone, pounding away at the computer keyboard. The model was jabbing away at his cell phone and pointedly ignoring Kyle. For his part, Kyle looked incredibly uncomfortable and was growing more and more fidgety with every passing moment. Jerry turned back to me, raising an eyebrow and getting his trademark evil smirk on his face. "Oh, I invited him, of course—the faux Antinous." Dani started to say something but Jerry acted like she wasn't even there and added, "His name is actually Jeremy Mikulak, but his professional name is Dirk Mantooth."

"You invited him," I replied, the wheels in my mind

spinning rapidly. I closed my eyes. "That's why you invited her in the first place, isn't it? You wanted to humiliate her publicly."

He got an overexaggerated innocent look on his face and sat back in his chair, raising his left hand to the base of his throat. "Moi?" He batted his eyelids at me. "Do you really think I would do such a thing?"

I closed my eyes. It all started to make sense. I'd never quite believed Jerry's rather lame excuses for including her in the program, which he had rigid control over. He'd also made it very clear that he despised Kyle Bennett. If I'd really thought about it—*give yourself a break, it's not like you haven't been stumbling over dead bodies ever since you got here*—I would have been more suspicious. If Jerry didn't like someone and didn't have a reason to be polite, that person simply didn't exist to him. Of course he'd had both Antinous—*Diana*—and Kyle come to Angels and Demons so he could have the model they'd paid to pretend to be her—*him*—show up and embarrass them. "You were planning an ambush, weren't you?"

"I thought it might be fun to have Jeremy show up at her and Kyle's panel today." His eyes glittered. "I thought it might make for some stimulating discussion—not your usual 'where do you get your ideas' stuff. The look on her face when she saw Jeremy would have more than worth the price of his plane ticket."

"You are *such* a bitch." Dani shook her head, but her tone was admiring. "That would have been brilliant."

Jerry graciously tilted his head in her direction. "Thank you. It would have been some pretty amazing theater, if I do say so myself."

"When did Jeremy get into town?" I reached into my purse for my phone.

Jerry gave me an odd look. "Why do you ask?"

"Why did you answer my question with another question?" I glanced over at the hostess table. They were still standing there. I fiddled with my phone, holding it under the table, swearing at myself. I am not good at technology and have never claimed to be. I avoided getting a smartphone for years, and I basically knew how to use a couple of the programs on my computers that I needed. Everything else was a mystery to me, but when I'd gotten my smartphone, the guy at the store had set me up with some kind of weird wireless "cloud" thing that was apparently something amazing. He'd explained it to me, but I hadn't really grasped much of anything he'd said other than I theoretically would no longer need to carry flash drives with me—every device I owned would be able to access the information available on the others as long as they were turned on.

So I should be able to access the photos Demi had taken with my phone.

"He flew in on Thursday morning," Jerry was saying. "One of his buddies from college lives in Gulfport, and he stayed over there until today. His friend brought him over, and I met him in the lobby."

"Do you think he killed Antinous?" Dani asked.

I touched the icon the guy in the store told me would allow me to access my computer files with my phone, then looked up. "I don't know if he did or he didn't. I was just curious." If the look on her face was any indication, she didn't believe me. "I'm not trying to solve anything, okay?" I glanced down and saw that several icons had popped up on the phone screen. I touched the one with the label *My Laptop,* and the little wheel started spinning. "I'm more than happy to leave that to the police." I smiled at Dani. "Or you, Dani."

She didn't say anything.

I turned back to Jerry. "And let me guess—not only were you going to surprise her with Antinous, you were going to have Anne Howard there, too—to complete the ambush?"

Jerry smiled back at me. "Guilty as charged." He shrugged. "The best-laid plans of mice and men."

She would have been utterly humiliated, I thought, and despite everything I knew about her, I couldn't help but feel a little sorry for her.

Then again, if you're going to be so nasty and hateful when you're at a keyboard in the safety of your own home, you should be prepared to have to defend yourself and your behavior in public. I hate people who grow a pair when they're behind a keyboard. I don't say anything on the Internet that I wouldn't say in person. "So, what now? The three of you are going to have a little lunch meeting? What's the point, now that she's dead? What are you up to, Jerry?"

"Kyle keeps pretending he didn't know anything about her deception," he replied with a scowl. "I don't believe him, and I'm sure Jeremy and I can get him to admit it."

"Why don't you join us?" I asked. "That way it won't look so much like an ambush. Besides, Dani is a TV reporter. I'm betting he'd love to get on TV." Dani shot me a grateful—and surprised—look. "We can have the waitress hold our entrees until yours are ready." I was already waving at our waitress.

A smile spread slowly across Jerry's face, and his right eyebrow went up. "Sure. Let me tell the hostess. Are you game, Dani?"

"Oh, yes." She reached into her purse and pulled out a digital recorder. "Let's do this."

Jerry got up and walked back over to the hostess stand as our waitress came back to our table. I explained to her the change in dining plans, and she nodded. "I'll let the kitchen know," she said.

After she left, Dani grabbed my hand on the table. "*Thank you for that.* I really want to get them both on camera—Jerry not so much—but between you, and them, we should be able to get the whole story! What a great exclusive! Hopefully we can get this all done in time for the evening news tomorrow night." She pulled out her phone and started tapping away on the screen.

While she was busy with her phone, I scrolled through the pictures Demi had taken. It was still impossible to tell who the man on the gallery was—the face was too well hidden, or just out of the shot—but the body? Maybe I could recognize him from the body.

I looked up as the hostess led the three men to our table. "Would you ladies follow me to another table?"

I got up, but Dani was still fiddling with her phone.

I bit my lower lip. I'd forgotten how dedicated she was to her career. Memory is a funny thing—for years, I'd been so completely focused on her betrayal while I was dealing with the deaths of my immediate family that it had slipped my mind that we'd had problems before all of that started. "Dani?" I said.

She didn't even look up as she kept typing away on her phone, but she did stand up and grab her purse.

"Dani, Tracy, this is Kyle Bennett and Jeremy Mikulak. Guys, Dani and Tracy," Jerry said, and we all murmured hellos before following the hostess to another, larger booth in another section of the restaurant.

The guys picked up their menus and Dani kept playing with her phone.

As I watched her thumbs flying over her screen, I remembered an argument we'd had several weeks before the accident that killed my parents. Dani had always been ambitious, which was one of the character traits of hers I really liked—well, at least at first. I wanted her to be successful. I wanted her to become the best damned television news reporter on the planet, to be honest. If she wanted to become the evening news anchor at one of the major networks or one of the cable channels, I would be right there at her side being as supportive as I could be. But then I began noticing little things that, by themselves, didn't bother me but overall added up to a particularly unpleasant picture of the woman I'd chosen to share my life with. Dani often missed my book signings and readings, claiming she was working on a story. That was fine—but whenever I had to miss something important to her because I was on deadline or really needed to get papers graded, she got angry with me and it almost always wound up with a fight if I didn't give in and do what she wanted. Often, I wouldn't even know she wasn't going to make an event of mine until she didn't actually show up there—and I got into the habit of making excuses for her: "Oh, she gets so nervous and tense for me that it becomes more stressful for me" or "Sorry, Dani's working on a story and not sure if she can make it, but she's going to try" so people wouldn't feel sorry for me. It had become so habitual that I did it without thinking.

Of course, it took Jerry to point this out to me. It was after a book signing at Garden District Books for either the third or fourth Laura Lassitter, and we were sitting on the porch at the Columns on St. Charles, watching as the daylight faded into twilight. "Why does Dani never come to any of your signings?" he asked, licking some salt off the rim of his margarita on the rocks. "It looks funny—and don't give me any of those bullshit excuses you fob everyone else off with. It's me, Jerry, you're talking to."

"She's working on a story," I replied, taking a sip from my heavenly Cosmo.

He made one of his patented faces at me—this one was "I said save the bullshit for someone else." "You know what I think? I think Dani has to be the center of attention, and she's not at your signings because she can't stand you getting all the attention instead of her, so she blows them off." He leaned back in his chair, a very smug look on his face. "And that should bother you. You're supposedly in a mutually beneficial relationship. You love and support her in her work. The least she can fucking do is show up at your signings to make an effort at supporting you."

That night, I mentioned this to her, just in passing—and it led to one of the nastiest fights of our time together. Dani was a master at turning things around, and somehow after the smoke cleared I found myself apologizing to her, just to bring it to a close so I could go to bed and get some sleep. But I'd spent the night staring at the ceiling, wondering why I always had to apologize, why she would never admit to being wrong under any circumstance, and why I didn't deserve better out of life than a partner who seemed to resent any success I might have.

The next morning, I was angry with myself for obsessing and for being so unsupportive of her. Jerry didn't like her, so he was hardly objective, after all.

But when my parents were killed to kick off what I would

eventually start referring to as the Time of Troubles, Jerry's words came back to haunt me, and I couldn't stop thinking about that argument. The resentments I'd been suppressing for years kept coming back to the surface every single time Dani wasn't there for me when I needed her—which was every time I needed her. As I schlepped over to the north shore to take my brother Michael to his doctor's appointments or to make sure he was taking his medications, lugging a laptop around with me everywhere so I could grade or work on my book or just to stay connected to a world outside this horrible world of misery I'd somehow slipped into that had no apparent end in sight, I wondered why I was having to do it alone. I wondered why she wasn't being emotionally supportive, why it was so hard for her to empathize with me and understand that sometimes I just needed nothing more than to vent or be held while I cried. I wondered why she couldn't help with some of the household chores, why there was never any food in the house unless I went to the grocery store, why the dirty clothes piled up in the laundry room, and why she never seemed to be around whenever I needed her.

Sometimes just a sympathetic hand on my shoulder when I was slumped over my laptop at the kitchen table would have been enough, would have meant the world to me, would have given me some strength from our relationship to draw from.

But she was too self-involved to even give me that little.

I glanced at her while the guys looked over the menus. She looked up from her phone and smiled at me. I forced myself to smile back at her, and she went back to her phone.

What had she said to me? That I'd shut her out, and that was why she'd turned to another woman?

I bit my lower lip. *Bullshit.* That was bullshit. She'd

always been selfish. Always. What I'd been going through was too much for her to deal with, so she'd turned her back on me. She then used what I was going through to justify her shitty behavior.

The bottom line was, really, what kind of a person cheats on their partner in that situation?

The kind of person I didn't want to be involved with.

Then again, she'd been through her own ordeal with Mary Digby dying.

Had she been there for her? Or had she closed herself off, found someone else to mess around with?

I hated myself for even wondering.

After the guys had ordered and the waitress had taken their menus away, I looked across the table at Jeremy Mikulak. *Here goes nothing,* I thought. "So, Jeremy, I have to ask—and I'm sure you must be really sick of being asked this—why did you agree to be the front man for Diana Browning? Surely she didn't have enough money to really make it worth your while?"

He hesitated for a moment. "It really sounds stupid now. I can't believe I was so dumb." Jeremy's face colored a little bit, and he looked down at his hands. He was good-looking, I supposed, if you were into men, with the short buzz cut, the green eyes, and the olive skin. I could tell from the creases in his cheeks that he had dimples when he smiled, and I could tell he had a worked-out physique, despite the baggy black T-shirt he was wearing. He was shorter than Kyle, who was maybe an inch or so shorter than me, so I figured that put Jeremy at maybe five-five—on a tall day with shoes on. His forearms were perfectly smooth, waxed clean of any recalcitrant body hair. He took a deep breath. "I was a dancer," he mumbled so quietly I could barely hear him over the hubbub in the restaurant. He glanced over at Jerry. "I was in college and dancing to pay the bills, you know how it is." He looked up again and spread his arms expressively in a what-else-was-I-supposed-to-do gesture.

Of course I knew from Jerry that "dancing" actually translated into "I was a stripper in gay bars."

Not that there was anything wrong with that—I could think of many worse ways to make money, and at least dancing for tips in your underwear wasn't against the law.

"And one night, this guy came up to me and put a twenty in my boots," he went on. "That really got my attention—you know guys don't give you that kind of money without… without, well, *you know*." He blushed even more deeply. "So, this guy didn't want anything for it, you know, just wanted to talk to me. So I went over to a corner of the bar and he gives me his business card. He worked for this publishing company called Belvedere Books—"

I resisted the urge to roll my eyes. Belvedere? As in Apollo Belvedere? Honestly.

"And they needed a good-looking guy to use for pictures for one of the authors. It was a woman author writing about gay men, and they needed a guy to pose for pictures and stuff they could use for her author pictures, for their website, and for the book covers and stuff. He offered me a thousand bucks to pose for the pictures, and a thousand bucks is a thousand bucks, so I said yes." He took a deep breath. "If I knew then what I know now."

"It wasn't as bad as that," Kyle said, squirming a bit in his seat.

"Shut up, Kyle, and let him finish." Jerry said it pleasantly enough, but there was just enough of a menacing undertone to his voice that Kyle shut up instantly. "Go on, Jeremy. Tell them what you told me."

"I didn't see any harm in it," he went on, a bit hesitantly. "Modeling is modeling, and the money was good, you know? And I wanted to be a writer—that's why I was going to school, to learn how to be a writer, and I figured, maybe if I get hooked up with this publisher maybe they'll give me a shot when I was ready? An in's an in, right? And my teachers always said that part of getting published was luck…sometimes you had to make connections, and this was a connection, right? So I took his card and gave him a call the next day. He had me come in and they made me an offer."

I realized I was clutching and twisting at my napkin with a death grip, and placed it on my lap. As a teacher and an author, nothing makes me angrier than con artists who prey on the dreams of those who are too naïve to know any better—especially when it comes to publishing. It was far too easy for me to look at someone like Jeremy and think, *That could have happened to me.*

"What was the offer?" I asked as Kyle continued to squirm in his seat.

"It was very simple. They would pay me a thousand dollars to pose for the pictures, and I signed an agreement." Jeremy took a deep breath. "Yes, I was stupid. I didn't read the agreement first." He glared at Kyle. "The agreement I signed also said I agreed to make public appearances as Antinous Renault, give interviews if necessary, sign books, do readings, all of it. It also had a confidentiality clause—if I violated the agreement, I was financially liable for damages." He shrugged. "So I posed for the pictures. It wasn't my first time in front of a camera—I'd done some modeling, too, in addition to the dancing—"

"Porn?" This was from Dani. I gave her a dirty look for interrupting—what difference did it make if he'd done porn? She refused to meet my eyes.

He nodded. "Yes, I did some porn. A couple of videos, all shot over one weekend. Does that matter?"

"It doesn't matter," I said. "So, what happened next?"

"The guy from the publisher—his name was Melvin Shannon—put me in touch with the woman I was fronting for, said she could help me with my writing. She was really nice—I only knew her as Antinous, that was her email address and how she signed her emails to me—and told me I had some raw ability, but needed some polishing." His face colored. "So, she kept giving me advice and having me send my stuff to her. And I was making the appearances, like I agreed to."

"Did it never occur to you that people were getting to know you as Antinous, and that might cause problems when you published your own stuff?" Dani asked.

He nodded. "I asked Melvin about it, but he told me it wasn't a big deal, no one really paid that much attention to things like that, and I could always say Antinous was a pseudonym."

He looked so miserable I couldn't help but feel sorry for him.

"But then you'd be associated with her work for the rest of your career," Jerry replied, giving Kyle a sidelong glance, "and why would you want *that* hanging over your head?"

"She was a good writer!" Kyle finally spoke. "She was!"

"I was wondering if you'd lost the power of speech," I said acidly. "So, where exactly do you fit into this miserable story of…oh, I don't even know what you'd call it." I waved a hand. "A con job?"

"Ah, yes, Kyle's role in all of this," Jerry said in a tone

that someone who didn't know him might take as a friendly one. I knew him too well to think that. "You see, many moons ago, ladies, Kyle started his own publishing company because no one would publish his work, right, Kyle?" He remained mute, his lips pressed tightly together, and nodded. "Melvin Shannon went belly-up; Belvedere went bankrupt and he skipped out, owing a lot of people money. Kyle had done some freelance editing work for Belvedere, and since he already had a publishing company, and here were all these authors whose books just went out of print or weren't going to be published, so he picked out the ones he thought would make the most money for him—and Antinous was one of them."

"I didn't want to keep the deception going," Kyle insisted. "I didn't! But Diana—Diana wanted to."

"Did she? Did she *really*?" Jerry purred. "Remember, Kyle, Dani's a reporter. This is going to go on the news. So think very carefully about your role in all of this, and what you're going to say." He leaned in closer. "And it's her job to verify *facts*."

Kyle opened and closed his mouth.

"Kyle contacted me." Jeremy took up his story again with a slight frown. "And told me he'd bought my contract from Belvedere, and that if I didn't keep pretending to be Antinous, he'd sue me." His face wrinkled in confusion. "They both told me I'd be blackballed if the truth ever came out, that no one would ever publish me if I caused so much trouble. And she stopped being so nice and encouraging." He rubbed his eyes. "Melvin had been kind of mean and nasty sometimes, but now? She was even meaner and nastier than he'd ever been. She threatened me. She told me if I didn't do what she told me to do, she'd make sure I'd never ever get anywhere as a writer. No agent would touch me, no publisher would come near me. She said she would ruin me if I didn't do what she told me to. And Kyle—" He shuddered. "You can sit there and act like you were innocent, Kyle, all you want to. You were in on it with her, all the way up to your neck. You could have put a stop to it at any time, but you didn't. You're a disgusting, miserable excuse for a human being." He made a face. "Kyle even offered to intercede with her for me, said he might be able to make it not so rough on me—if I slept with him."

We all looked at Kyle. I didn't even try to disguise my utter contempt. "How repugnant," I said after digesting it for a moment. I was revolted—this whole sordid story made my skin crawl. "This is kind of like the whole Milli Vanilli thing, only with books." I got a blank look from Jeremy, so I explained, "They were a couple of models who were hired to front a singing group, only they lip-synced for the real singers who weren't as pretty as they were because the record company didn't think the real singers would make it on their own talent. It was a big scandal in the early 1990s."

"But everyone lip-syncs now," he replied, frowning.

"Believe it or not, dear, there used to be a time when singers were not only expected to sing live but they were also expected to sound good," Jerry said, patting Jeremy's shoulder and smiling at him.

"So I didn't know what to do," Jeremy went on finally. "And then Anne Howard found me…and the rest is history." He scowled. "All along, they'd been lying to me. They didn't have a leg to stand on. They *blackmailed* me into going along with their fraud."

"That isn't how it started," Kyle blurted out. He looked absolutely miserable—and I was kind of glad. The whole story was more disgusting than I could have ever possibly imagined.

Had I known any of this when she'd sat down next to me at the airport Thursday, I would have slapped her senseless.

"Tell them, Kyle," Jerry said sharply. "Tell them everything."

"Jerry was right about my book." Kyle took a deep breath. "No one would publish it. No agent would represent it. I got some money when my grandfather died, so I started my own press and self-published it. It got good reviews...it didn't sell very well, but it got good reviews."

"On Amazon." Jerry made a face.

"Yes, on Amazon!" Kyle snapped. "I wanted to work in publishing so badly, wanted to be a writer so badly...but no one wanted to publish me or hire me. I am talented, goddamnit! But I lost my shirt on my collection—didn't even earn back its cost. So I started doing some work for Belvedere. It was located in Baltimore, where I'm from, and I...I had a crush on Antinous," he mumbled, turning dark scarlet. "Jeremy did a signing at the gay bookstore in Baltimore, and so I went."

"Because you wanted to meet Antinous?" This was from Dani. "Because you thought he was hot."

He nodded. His face was so red his pimples stood out in bas relief. "I talked to him about the book, but it was weird—he couldn't answer some basic questions I had about the book, and it was so obvious, in the bio and everything, that he was British and older, so I started getting suspicious. I did a little research—it wasn't that hard, he told me he was still a student at the University of Maryland—I was right, he wasn't British at all. And I found out who he really was...and then I knew. I knew he hadn't written those books. I tracked down Melvin and confronted him. He admitted everything. He offered me a job editing, offered to publish my next book." Kyle swallowed. "And when Melvin went bankrupt, I took over his list and his authors. I borrowed money. My press was doing well, you know—I was right, I knew what I was doing. I kept telling her to calm down, play it cool, pull back and not be so nasty publicly about other authors on her website." His voice shook. "And she kept telling me she owed it to the readers, and the genre, to be honest, to tip them off to bad books and bad authors—she made it sound noble."

"Bullshit," Jerry said pleasantly. "She was your hit woman. You used her as a mouthpiece to get even with authors you felt had slighted you." He crossed his arms. "You're just as big a piece of filth as she ever was. You didn't turn on her until it started hurting your wallet. You reveled in her nastiness." He turned to me. "Remember how I told you she went after me? I emailed Kyle—but that wasn't personal, was it, Kyle? It wasn't because I'd refused to blurb one of your books, was it? She just thought my book sucked, didn't she?" He laughed. "She was such a fucking egomaniac, and Kyle, you're no better than she is."

I have thousands of fans, I heard her smug voice telling me at the airport again.

"So I did a little digging of my own," Jerry went on. "I found out what her real name was, everything—it really wasn't hard, she wasn't smart enough to cover her tracks that well. Anyone could have found out Antinous was actually a woman pretending to be a man." He rolled his eyes theatrically. "So of course, when she went after Leslie MacKenzie, I got in touch with Anne Howard. The rest was history."

"She was so defiant," Kyle went on, swallowing hard. "She blamed everyone else but wouldn't take any responsibility herself. It was everyone else's fault—she blamed *me* for wanting to keep the deception going."

"And you denied everything?" I raised my eyebrows.

"You claimed you didn't know she was really a woman?" I shook my head. "You were telling *her* to come clean while you lied?"

"I didn't know what to do," he pleaded, his voice getting higher and whinier. "Her next book was already in production. I couldn't pull it and lose the money. I was bleeding money left and right. I didn't know what I was going to do."

I exchanged a grim look with Jerry.

"When Anne Howard got in touch with me, I told her the truth," Jeremy replied with a sigh. "I was tired of all the lies, and I just didn't care anymore. If it meant I wasn't going to ever be an author, so be it. I was sick of everything. Anne told me that her threats were just that, empty threats, and that there wasn't really a damned thing she could do. That I'd been just stupid and she'd used me. And she offered to help me get out from under her. It was such a relief to not have to lie anymore! To be able to tell the truth finally." He slumped down a bit in his seat. "I feel like such an idiot."

"You shouldn't," I said slowly, meeting Jerry's eyes. "You were manipulated and used. Don't blame yourself for trusting the wrong people."

Wheels in my head were turning, everything I'd been told and seen and heard over the past few days trying to come together in my head. *Think of it as the plot of a book, and try to make sense of it that way.*

"So, Jerry, you invited everyone involved to come to Angels and Demons?" Dani asked.

He nodded. Dani's eyes looked like they were about to pop out of her head, and I could see the wheels turning in her head, repeating over and over *Big story, big story, big story!*

And of course, that was what really mattered to her. But now wasn't the time to say anything.

"So I suppose the only question left is who killed her," I said bitterly. "And poor Demi."

"Can I interview you on camera, Jeremy?" Dani already had her cell phone in her hand. "You, too, Kyle. I'm betting I can get this on the national broadcast." Ambition glittered in her eyes. She got up and walked away from the table, leaving the four of us alone as she called her producer.

Yeah, well, you knew deep down it was going to end this way, I thought as I watched her walk back out into the lobby of the hotel, then turned back to look at the three gay men at my table. "So which one of you bitches murdered Antinous?"

Kyle and Jeremy both stared at me, but Jerry burst into raucous laughter. After a few moments, he got hold of himself and smiled at me. "I love you so much."

"Yes, well." I took a bite out of my cheeseburger. I was chewing when it all became clear to me.

How could I have been so blind?

CHAPTER ELEVEN

D ani was good at her job, I'll give her that.
Within an hour, she had an entire news production team at the hotel and was set up in one of the conference rooms on the mezzanine lobby. Jerry had helped, getting in touch with his hotel conference planner to get the keys and get the room opened up. He was being so incredibly helpful to her and not in the least bit snarky—which of course had my antennae up. He also, with some help from his volunteers, had assembled everyone who had anything to do with the story in another room, just down the hall from the conference room—and had catering bring up coffee and water for everyone.

Kyle Bennett was sweating, even though the room was cold. Demi's friends were all huddled together, whispering to each other. Leslie MacKenzie was sitting next to her son, and they both looked like they'd rather be anywhere else. Kenny Simon stood, leaning on the back wall, glaring at Kyle.

And, of course, Jerry was there, a smirk on his face.

I poured myself a cup of coffee and looked around the room, and couldn't help but laugh a bit to myself inwardly.

This is such a scene from a classic mystery—all the suspects gathered in one room. I could never get away with this in one of my books! The only thing missing is the cop.

And as if on cue, Detective Randisi walked into the room. He smiled when he saw me and joined me at the sideboard.

"Coffee?" I asked.

He shook his head. "Figured it all out yet?" The corners of his mouth twitched.

"I think so," I replied with a shrug. I looked around the room and cleared my throat.

Everyone's heads swiveled in my direction.

"Thank you all for coming," I said, managing somehow to keep my voice steady. "I think we all know each other, so introductions aren't necessary. On behalf of Dani, I'd like to thank you for agreeing to be interviewed for her story. I know we are all curious as to what's been going on around here this weekend. Who killed Antinous, and who killed Demi." I glanced over at Demi's friends, who still looked a bit shell-shocked. "I believe I've figured out everything now that has happened, and while we wait to go on camera with Dani, I'm going to float my theory past all of you." Every eye turned to me. "Okay, let's get started." I took a deep breath. "Okay. What most people here don't know is that Demi loved to use her camera phone. She loved to document everything she did, posting the pictures on Facebook." Her friends nodded. "So, when Demi arrived at the Maison Maintenon on Thursday, she got her phone out and took pictures of her room. She also took pictures of the *view* from her room."

Randisi smiled. "According to the Maison Maintenon, she arrived from the airport and checked into her room around two thirty."

"So, give or take, she started taking pictures around

three-ish." I shrugged. "She got here before her friends, who arrived later in the day. Her room was on the third floor of the main building at the Maison Maintenon, with two big French windows that looked out onto the pool in the back courtyard. So when she was taking pictures of the pool, she was *also* taking pictures of the gallery of the slave quarter. I don't think she was really paying any attention to the gallery behind the pool—she was too busy taking pictures. She was on vacation, here to learn about writing and make some connections in the industry, she was away from her family…she wanted to have a good time. And of course document every little bit of her trip. What she didn't know was that she actually got pictures of a man going to Antinous's room. I don't even know if she noticed at the time she took the pictures. At any rate, she was taking pictures that showed not only the gallery, but also part of the door to Antinous's room. The gallery roof cut off part of the view, but she managed to get pictures of a man at Antinous's door before the time she was actually murdered. And I don't think she realized what she had pictures of—not until she downloaded them into her laptop the next day. Once she looked at the pictures, she knew what she had—but at the same time she wasn't really sure if it meant anything or not. And the man in the pictures did not know that he'd been photographed."

"She took pictures of the killer?" This was Pat, and her voice was shaking. "Oh my God."

"I didn't say that," I replied. "I said she took pictures of a man going to Antinous's room." I closed my eyes. "But those pictures are significant because those pictures *are* the reason why Demi was murdered." I opened my eyes and looked around the room. "I've been confused and had difficulty figuring out everything that happened over the past few days because, you see, I, and the police, have assumed all along the two murders were committed by the same person and were linked. I assumed the man in Demi's pictures had killed Antinous, and then when he found out about the pictures, he killed Demi. And we were both right and wrong about the link."

"How can you be right and wrong?" This was Leslie MacKenzie. Sitting next to her son, she leaned forward curiously. "You can't be both."

"In this case, yes, we can," I replied. "You see, the murders *are* linked—but not in the way I and Detective Randisi and everyone assumed. If Antinous had not been murdered, Demi would still be alive. But they were killed by different people, and for different reasons." I shook my head. "Demi took a picture of someone going into Antinous's room before Antinous was murdered, and then Demi herself was murdered. It stood to reason that Antinous's murderer and Demi's murderer were one and the same. But it wasn't the case. Demi *was* killed because of the pictures she took, *but she didn't take a picture of Antinous's murderer.*" I turned to Leslie MacKenzie. "But you didn't know that, did you, Leslie?"

Every eye in the room turned to Leslie MacKenzie, who looked confused. "I don't know what you're talking about."

"It's okay, Leslie," I said reassuringly. "Any mother would have done what you did. Those pictures Demi took—that was your son, wasn't it?"

Lance turned and stared at his mother. "Mom?"

"She recognized him," Leslie replied. "She walked back with me from the Monteleone Hotel back to the Maison Maintenon yesterday afternoon. She came running after me on Royal Street. She told me she had something to show me, about Lance, that I'd want to know." Her voice shook, her eyes filling with tears. "When she showed me the pictures on her laptop, and I saw Lance…I just grabbed the laptop out of her hands and hit her with it, God help me, I didn't know what I was doing, I swear…and then when I saw she was dead and the laptop was destroyed…I just got the hell out of there."

"But, Mom, I didn't kill that awful woman!" Lance grabbed her hands. "You have to believe me!" He turned back to me and Randisi. "I didn't kill her!"

I nodded. "I know. You just went to confront her, didn't you? You just wanted to give her a piece of your mind."

"Yes." He nodded. "I didn't know what I was going to do, honestly. I really didn't, but I wanted to see her, face-to-face, have her look me in the eye and say the things she'd said about me and my mother to my face. But she wasn't there. I knocked and knocked and she never answered, so I went back to my own room." He swallowed. "I just assumed I'd run into her later."

"She didn't answer." I picked up my narrative again. "She couldn't answer because not only was she not in her room— she was already dead." I turned back to Randisi with a smile. "You didn't find a murder weapon in her room, did you?"

He shook his head. "No, we didn't find anything in her room that could have been used to kill her. There was no blood, nothing. She wasn't killed in her room."

"That was the first problem," I went on. "Everyone *assumed* she'd been killed in her room, and the killer panicked and tossed her body over the gallery railing. That was a conundrum for me. She wasn't a small woman, so I could not for the life of me figure how the killer had gotten her over that railing." I shook my head. "Which of course was all wrong. The killer didn't get her over the railing because the killer didn't need to. That was the other thing I was wrong about." I sighed. "It all had to do with the layout of the hotel—but it's funny how you can convince yourself about something and you don't see the obvious. I was operating under the assumption all along that the killer had killed Antinous in the heat of the moment and then tossed her over the railing because he panicked. I was so blind. Antinous didn't come over the railing. She came out of a window on the third floor of the slave quarters." I laughed at myself. "I was so stupid. This wasn't a spur-of-the-moment murder. This was carefully planned, almost from the very beginning.

"Any number of people had reason to want her dead. She was an incredibly unpleasant woman—arrogant, self-absorbed, she wandered through life like a bull in a china shop, carelessly causing damage everywhere she blundered and bumbled. And she didn't care. She always excused herself, found a way to blame someone else for what she'd done. When the killer found out she was coming to Angels and Demons, the killer started planning this out. The great irony of it all is that Antinous herself, in her own arrogance, gave the killer all the information needed to commit the crime. Some of it was, of course, just blind luck. The killer couldn't have known, of course, that Antinous's room was going to be directly below hers—that was just a stroke of really good luck."

"Hers?" Jerry asked, incredulous.

"Hers." I nodded. "Why would you need to toss Antinous over the railing if you killed her in her room? You wouldn't. You could just leave the body there and lock the door behind you on your way out. Housekeeping would find her the next morning—and no one would be the wiser. It was very dramatic. I couldn't make sense of it, really. She was heavy, over three hundred pounds. Why do it? And then I realized, *What if she*

wasn't killed in her room? What if, in fact, she was in someone else's room? And then the proverbial lightbulb came on over my head. The killer was, in fact, getting rid of the body. It was the easiest way to do it. It was a stroke of luck for the killer that her room just happened to be directly over Antinous's."

"Why not just kill her in her room?"

"Because of *evidence*," I replied. "There would be evidence that the killer had been there in her room. No matter how careful you are, you always leave something behind— that's how killers get caught, usually. Someone might see you. No, the killer's plan had always been to lure Antinous to her room, kill her, and then get rid of the body by dumping it out the window. In a place like the Maintenon, where every room has a balcony or opens out into a gallery or has a big window, it would be easy. I thought I heard a door open right before the body came down. It wasn't an actual door, but *French windows*. The third floor of the slave quarters has a gallery on the other side, but has French doors that open out into the pool courtyard. I heard the doors open, and a grunt as the killer shoved the body out. I—and everyone else—assumed it was Antinous's door opening because her room was directly above where her body landed. Antinous's door was locked, but we all assumed the killer had locked and closed the door after tossing the body over the railing. But why would the killer do that? I didn't hear anyone walking along the gallery afterward—I assumed that when I screamed, that drowned it all out. But I didn't hear footsteps because there weren't any to hear." I turned to Pat. "Isn't that right, Pat? Your room—that is, your *other* hotel room—was directly above Antinous's. You lured her up to your room, you killed her, and then you shoved her body out the French doors after making sure no one was looking."

Pat's face went white. "I'm not saying anything until I speak to a lawyer."

"But why would Pat kill her?" This was from Kyle Bennett.

"The one player in the entire scandal of Antinous's real identity that isn't here is Anne Howard." I turned back to Pat. "This whole thing has hinged on identities, hidden and secret personas. I did a web search on Anne Howard. Like Antinous, no pictures anywhere online. I started wondering, who the hell is this Anne Howard, anyway? Why did she hate Antinous so much? When Leslie told me at the party last night that she and Anne had never actually met, this afternoon I realized, *If Antinous Renault was a pseudonym, why couldn't Anne Howard be one as well?* Then all I had to do was have Detective Randisi check with the Maison Maintenon…and sure enough, Anne Howard's room was above Antinous's. It all clicked into place. Pat had made it very clear to me Friday morning in the coffee shop she hated Antinous. She engaged with me on purpose at the coffee shop, to find out what I'd heard and what I knew. I told her what I believed at the time to be true…and she thought she'd gotten away with it."

"But why?" Ted asked. "Why would she do it?"

"I have a pretty good idea about that, too." I leaned against the wall. "She stole your work, didn't she?"

"I want a lawyer," Pat hissed through clenched teeth. "You can't prove any of this."

"What do you mean, she stole her work?" Jerry was goggling at me.

"*Why* did Anne Howard hate Antinous so much?" I asked rhetorically. "Anne Howard wasn't a writer, she didn't really exist rather than as a blog where she reviewed books. But if you read through her blog—which I did—from the very beginning, she hated Antinous. Her very first blog is a really in-depth attack on her. When I thought about it, I began to wonder, and the more I thought, the more I wondered. Anne Howard's only reason for existence was to attack Antinous. She was the one who exposed her to the world as a fraud... and in the earliest blog entries, one of the crimes she accused Antinous of was plagiarism. Antinous herself didn't understand why Anne Howard hated her so much—it puzzled her, and with her enormous ego and desire to be loved by everyone, she tried to understand it. Of course, it never occurred to Antinous that Anne Howard and Pat Greenleaf were the same person. Isn't that right, Pat? In the coffee shop the other morning you called Antinous a plagiarist. The only other person to make that accusation was Anne Howard." I shrugged. "It doesn't really matter. Once the police search your room and do tests, they'll find evidence that Antinous actually died there."

The cops came in, arrested both Pat and Leslie, and took them away in cuffs.

"Now I need a drink," I said to the rest of the room.

"It's on me," Jerry said.

I was on my third margarita when Dani came into the bar, looking for me. Jerry nodded and got up. "I'll talk to you later," he said, and walked away.

"What a scoop!" Dani shook her head as she sat down.

"I can't believe you said 'scoop,'" I replied.

"The story's going national." She grinned at me, putting her hand on top of mine. "Are you sure you don't want to go in front of the cameras?"

I shook my head. "I don't want the publicity." My agent Mabel and the PR person at my publisher would slap me silly, but there was no reason for them to ever know. "The last thing I want or need is to be called Jessica Fletcher." I shuddered. "No thanks."

"But for me, the big story is us." She looked deep into my eyes. "I'm so glad we're back together."

I cleared my throat. "Yeah. About that." I took a deep breath. "I'm not so sure that's a good idea."

Her jaw dropped.

Yes, Dani, you're not used to not getting what you want, are you?

"We had problems even before you cheated on me, Dani," I said carefully. "And I'm not sure I want to pick up where we left off. I live on the north shore, you still live in New Orleans, and your career is always going to come first." I held up my hand as she started to sputter. "Let me finish. I'm not ruling it out—but we need to go slow, get to know each other again. I think we went too fast the first time. Let's date first." I stood up. "I won't be back down to Louisiana for another week or so, anyway. Let's think about it, decide what we want. I'll call you when I get back home and settled."

A smile crept across her face. "You're going to make me work for it, aren't you?"

I couldn't help but smile back. "Something like that, yeah." I leaned down and kissed her cheek. "I'll call you, okay?"

"But when are you heading back up north?"

"My flight's tomorrow afternoon—but I have a book to finish." I touched her cheek lightly with my fingers. "I will call you."

She nodded. "I look forward to hearing from you."

I whistled as I walked to the elevator.

About the Author

Valerie Bronwen is a retired journalist and former writing instructor from New Orleans. Her first published short story, "The Other Side of the Mirror," appeared in the anthology *Women of the Dark Streets*. Valerie is a longtime fan of the mystery genre. *Slash and Burn* is her first novel, and she is working on a follow-up in her home on Coliseum Square in New Orleans.

Books Available From Bold Strokes Books

Wingspan by Karis Walsh. Wildlife biologist Bailey Chase is content to live at the wild bird sanctuary she has created on Washington's Olympic Peninsula until she is lured beyond the safety of isolation by architect Kendall Pearson. (978-1-60282-983-1)

Night Bound by Winter Pennington. Kass struggles to keep her head, her heart, and her relationships in order. She's still having a difficult time accepting being an Alpha female—but her wolf is certain of what she wants and she's intent on securing her power. (978-1-60282-984-8)

The Blush Factor by Gun Brooke. Ice-cold business tycoon Eleanor Ashcroft only cares about the three Ps—Power, Profit, and Prosperity—until young Addison Garr makes her doubt both that and the state of her frostbitten heart. (978-1-60282-985-5)

Slash and Burn by Valerie Bronwen. The murder of a roundly despised author at a LGBT writers' conference in New Orleans turns Winter Lovelace's relaxing weekend hobnobbing with her peers into a nightmare of suspense—especially when her ex turns up. (978-1-60282-986-2)

The Quickening: A Sisters of Spirits novel by Yvonne Heidt. Ghosts, visions, and demons are all in a day's work for Tiffany. But when Kat asks for help on a serial killer case, life takes on another dimension altogether. (978-1-60282-975-6)

Windigo Thrall by Cate Culpepper. Six women trapped in a mountain cabin by a blizzard, stalked by an ancient cannibal demon bent on stealing their sanity—and their lives. (978-1-60282-950-3)

Smoke and Fire by Julie Cannon. Oil and water, passion and desire, a combustible combination. Can two women fight the fire that draws them together and threatens to keep them apart? (978-1-60282-977-0)

Love and Devotion by Jove Belle. KC Hall trips her way through life, stumbling into an affair with a married bombshell twice her age. Thankfully, her best friend, Emma Reynolds, is there to show her the true meaning of Love and Devotion. (978-1-60282-965-7)

The Shoal of Time by J.M. Redmann. It sounded too easy. Micky Knight is reluctant to take the case because the easy ones often turn into the hard ones, and the hard ones turn into the dangerous ones. In this one, easy turns hard without warning. (978-1-60282-967-1)

In Between by Jane Hoppen. At the age of fourteen, Sophie Schmidt discovers that she was born an intersexual baby and sets off on a journey to find her place in a world that denies her true existence. (978-1-60282-968-8)

Under Her Spell by Maggie Morton. The magic of love brought Terra and Athene together, but now a magical quest stands between them— a quest for Athene's hand in marriage. Will their passion keep them together, or will stronger magic tear them apart? (978-1-60282-973-2)

Scars by Amy Dunne. While fleeing from her abuser, Nicola Jackson bumps into Jenny O'Connor, and their unlikely friendship quickly develops into a blossoming romance—but when it comes down to a matter of life or death, are they both willing to face their fears? (978-1-60282-970-1)

Rush by Carsen Taite. Murder, secrets, and romance combine to create the ultimate rush. (978-1-60282-966-4)

Homestead by Radclyffe. R. Clayton Sutter figures getting NorthAm Fuel's newest refinery operational on a rolling tract of land in upstate New York should take a month or two, but then, she hadn't counted on local resistance in the form of vandalism, petitions, and one furious farmer named Tess Rogers. (978-1-60282-956-5)

Battle of Forces: Sera Toujours by Ali Vali. Kendal and Piper return to New Orleans to start the rest of eternity together, but the return of an old enemy makes their peaceful reunion short-lived, especially when they join forces with the new queen of the vampires. (978-1-60282-957-2)

How Sweet It Is by Melissa Brayden. Some things are better than chocolate. Molly O'Brien enjoys her quiet life running the bakeshop in a small town. When the beautiful Jordan Tuscana returns home, Molly can't deny the attraction—or the stirrings of something more. (978-1-60282-958-9)

The Missing Juliet: A Fisher Key Adventure by Sam Cameron. A teenage detective and her friends search for a kidnapped Hollywood star in the Florida Keys. (978-1-60282-959-6)

Amor and More: Love Everafter, edited by Radclyffe and Stacia Seaman. Rediscover favorite couples as Bold Strokes Books authors reveal glimpses of life and love beyond the honeymoon in short stories featuring main characters from favorite BSB novels. (978-1-60282-963-3)

First Love by CJ Harte. Finding true love is hard enough, but for Jordan Thompson, daughter of a conservative president, it's challenging, especially when that love is a female rodeo cowgirl. (978-1-60282-949-7)

Pale Wings Protecting by Lesley Davis. Posing as a couple to investigate the abduction of infants, Special Agent Blythe Kent and Detective Daryl Chandler find themselves drawn into a battle over the innocents, with demons on one side and the unlikeliest of protectors on the other. (978-1-60282-964-0)